His eyes were so very blue. Blue like a deep blue sky, they mesmerized me.

"You're here," I murmured, my voice barely audible.

He ran a hand along the slope of my cheek. "And you," he said simply.

"How?"

"I've heard it said that Mackinac Island has a kind of magic."

His words sent a shiver along my spine. I'd heard that as well. I thought it was the water of the lake sweeping against the sandy shore. The mournful cry of the ferry as it came and went, taking people to and from this island that seemed to be stuck in time where cars weren't allowed. Where people traveled by horse and buggy instead of fancy cars.

That, I'd thought, was the magic.

But if Cody was here, then the magic was something else.

Sealed with a Kiss

ALSO BY KATHRYN KALEIGH

Contemporary Romance
The Worthington Family

The Lady in the Red Dress

On the Edge of Chance

Sealed with a Kiss

Kiss me at Midnight

Billionaire's Unexpected Landing

Billionaire's Accidental Girlfriend

Billionaire Fallen Angel

Billionaire's Secret Crush

Billionaire's Barefoot Bride

The Heart of Christmas

The Magic of Christmas

In a One Horse Open Sleigh

A Secret Royal Christmas

An Old-Fashioned Christmas

Second Chance Kisses

Second Chance Secrets

First Time Charm

Three Broken Rules

Second Chance Destiny

Unexpected Vows

Begin Again

Love Again

Falling Again

Just Stay

Just Chance

Just Believe

Just Us

Just Once

Just Happened

Just Maybe

Just Pretend

Just Because

Sealed with a Kiss

THE WORTHINGTONS

KATHRYN KALEIGH

SEALED WITH A KISS

KISS ME AT MIDNIGHT PREVIEW

To learn more about Kathryn Kaleigh, visit

www.kathrynkaleigh.com

Kathryn Kaleigh

Prologue

Amelia

1815

With the moon no more than a sliver, a scattered array of stars, tossed against the inky sky, were bright tonight.

It was a lovely spring evening, chilly following the warmth of day. One of those evenings when lightning bugs sparkled as they left the ground to make their way into the trees.

Inside her house along the shore of Lake Huron, Amelia moved from the window where other than fireflies, she saw little more than the faint glow of the lighthouse across the water.

Pausing to study a painting on the wall, Amelia bit her lip and contemplated whether it should be moved to the other side of the room where she could see it while she drank her tea at breakfast.

The painting was a rather nice likeness of her and her new husband, Carlton.

Carlton was breathtakingly handsome in his British uniform and Amelia looked lovely in her wedding gown. They had been so very young. Barely out of leading strings, they had been consumed with that first blush of love reserved only for the young.

The painting had been done in England, just days after their wedding, and right before Carlton sailed for America. That the painting had survived the voyage was a miracle in and of itself.

Carlton had said he would build her a house and build her a house he did.

He'd come here with the British soldiers to fight in what became known as the War of 1812.

After the capture of Fort Mackinac, Carlton had sworn his allegiance to America and sent for his wife. He built this house while she traveled, but he had been called back before she arrived.

They had been like two ships passing in the night.

She received a letter just two weeks ago that he would be home by the end of June.

The end of June had come and gone.

But Carlton had not returned.

With every knock at the door her heart leapt with hope that it might be Carlton.

But when the knock came tonight after the sun had already set, she knew even before she reached the door that it was not Carlton.

"Hello," she said, opening the door to the soldier waiting on the other side of the door.

"Mrs. Winters?"

He was a kind man, young. Much as Amelia and Carlton had been when they had wed. After delivering the letter, he had left her alone again.

Taking the letter with her, she went sit on the sofa, the painting on the wall in front of her.

She sat there, holding it in her hands, staring at the images in shadows on the wall. After some time, after the clock chimed the hour, she pulled a candle close and slipped her finger beneath the fold, breaking the wax seal on the envelope. A seal she did not recognize.

Carlton was not coming home. He had been lost at sea.

She sat there, thinking nothing and everything for hours. She didn't cry. She hardly felt anything other than an odd numbness.

It was after the clock struck Midnight and the candle had sputtered out that Amelia managed to drag herself from the couch.

She went to her writing desk, uncorked a bottle of ink, and began to write.

> My dearest Carlton,
> They tell me you were lost at sea.
> But I want you to know that I will never give up on you.
> If there is the remotest chance that you could still be out there somewhere, I will wait for you.
> Know that I will stay here at this house. Until the end of time. And I will wait for you.
> I will wait because true love never dims.
> Your truest love,
> Amelia

Leaving the letter out for the ink to dry, she dragged herself upstairs and, not even bothering to undress, crawled beneath the blankets.

She didn't wake up.

She died that night of takotsubo syndrome.

A broken heart.

CHAPTER 1

Bailey Winters

DARK BLUE WATER, lapping against the sandy shore, stretched to the horizon where it blended into a hazy band, then blossomed into a light blue sky with fluffy fair weather cumulus clouds drifting lazily.

A faint glow from the top of the lighthouse just out from the water's edge deferred its warning sentinel to the bright mid-morning sunlight.

Standing at my floor to ceiling living room window, I watched as a ferry, a tall spray of water following in its wake, sailed its way across Lake Huron. The ferry would be packed with early season tourists coming out to spend the day on Mackinac Island. As the ferry neared the island, the mournful wail of its horn echoed across the water.

It was still hard to think of myself as anything other than a tourist.

My living room.

I came from a small family. No siblings. No cousins. My mother's older sister, Aunt Meagan, never married, but she'd knocked her career out of the park.

Started her own marketing company. Worked freelance. Made a stellar reputation for herself.

I visited her often in the summers when I was in high school. She'd spent a little time with me, but mostly she worked. She'd always made it a point to spend a few hours every afternoon with me, an early dinner, then she'd park me in front of the television and go back to her computer.

Sometimes I would slip out and walk down the sidewalk along the shore to downtown Mackinac. I'd just sit on a bench and watch people with the fascination of a teenager. I'd wondered what it would be like to be here on this romantic island with a boyfriend. I imagined how we'd get ice cream and watch the sunset.

But Aunt Meagan. She had worked hard. She'd been very successful.

She'd died far too young and as far as I knew, alone.

It was not a happy story for her.

I'd learned from her. I'd learned how to be successful and work hard. But I had also learned the importance of taking time off.

I'd learned, from Aunt Meagan's way of life, the importance of family.

I'd dated, seriously, one guy in college. After we'd split up, I had pretty much avoided relationships. Just because it was my fault, didn't make it hurt any less.

Then just when my life seemed to be settling in for the long haul, Aunt Meagan had gone and left me this house on Mackinac Island.

I was only twenty-six. Too young to live on this island alone. Or so I had thought until I got here.

There was a magic on Mackinac island. I'd always attributed it to the fancifulness of youth. Since I hadn't been here since I was seventeen, I saw it differently through my adult eyes.

Now as an adult, I knew it had not just been my childhood imagination. It really was magical.

Maybe it was the view. Maybe it was the cool air blended with the bright sunshine. Maybe it was the way the tourists carefreely rode their bicycles up and down the path along the lakeshore.

But still, I packed. I packed up a woman's life. A woman who had a successful career. Had she been lonely, I wondered? Or content in her own world?

Holding a roll of packing tape in one hand, I leaned against the window frame and watched an airplane approach the island. It was a small jet. A Cessna.

My college boyfriend, an aviation major, had been into airplanes and had loved to tell me all about them.

I didn't care about airplanes, but I cared that he cared. And whether I had wanted it to or not, information had soaked in. I was like that. A sponge, my father called me.

The ringing of a phone startled me. I checked my cell, but that wasn't it. Then I remembered.

My aunt, oddly enough, still had her landline. The same phone number she'd had for years.

I already fielded a couple of phone calls—that had been unpleasant to say the least.

"Hello?" I always answered my aunt's phone with a question.

There was silence for a moment.

"This is Betty from Houston. Is Meagan available?"

Taking the cordless phone with me, I dropped onto the sofa. I hated, hated doing this. Explaining to people that Aunt Meagan wasn't here anymore. I could say the words now, without emotion. I suppose I had developed some self-protective numbness.

"Give me a minute and I'll call you back," Betty from Houston, her voice a little hoarse, said after I finished my narrative.

As I sat there waiting for her to call back, I stared at the painting on the wall in front of me. The painting had been here in this same spot for as long as I could remember. It was a faded painting of a young couple. A man in his uniform and a young lady in what I always imagined to be her wedding gown.

Even in the faded black and white painting, I could see the happiness the artist had captured in their eyes.

Five minutes later, Betty from Houston called back.

"Sometimes your aunt rented out her guest room to my employees."

Did I know that? There was a guest room behind the kitchen and now that I thought about it, it was obviously for guests. It hadn't occurred to me to consider what guests.

"I didn't really know that," I said. "Employees?"

"Worthington Enterprises," Betty said. "Not all the time. Just a night or two here and there."

"Okay." While I'd been going through my aunt's things, I'd noticed some odd notations that now made sense.

Maybe it was how she kept from being lonely.

At any rate, it was time to tackle Aunt Meagan's financial records. I needed to be sure.

"But I need it for six months this time," Betty said. She named off an amount that left me momentarily speechless.

"We pay ahead and I can transfer the money electronically to your account."

"Okay," I said. The amount would cover my apartment rent in Dallas for at least two years. I gave her my cell phone number that linked to my bank account.

"Great," Betty from Houston said. "I don't know which of my guys it will be yet, but I'll go ahead and send over the money to reserve the room."

Just minutes after we disconnected, I had a notice on my phone that the full amount she named had just been deposited in my account.

The guest could rent the whole house for that amount. I'd be out of here soon anyway.

Nine days later, however, I was still here.

At the time Betty from Houston had called, I figured I'd rent out the room, put the house on the market, and go back to my life in Dallas.

But I was still here.

And I'd somehow, through the process of setting up my own work area in my aunt's upstairs office, gotten comfortable working here.

I was inspired by the view of the lake that looked more like an ocean. The white birds that dipped down into the water and back up, often times with a fish in their beaks.

Found comfort in watching the neighbor who walked his white Siberian Husky every morning at seven o'clock. And again in the evenings. Sometimes he tossed a stick into the water for the dog to chase after. Sometimes, when it was cold, they would just walk down the sidewalk, then hurry back home to the warmth of their own home.

Maybe it was the horse and buggies, in lieu of automobiles, that passed by on the road below. There were no cars on Mackinac and that had always been something that I found to be enchanting in and of itself.

There were only two ways to get on and off Mackinac Island. By ferry or by airplane.

CHAPTER 2
Cody Johnson

A TYPICAL WEDNESDAY morning for a flight.

The early morning sun streamed in through the cockpit window on the right, glancing off the computer screens in front of me.

The horizon stretched for miles in every direction, the blue sky blending into land. It looked like an artist had taken a brush and blurred the horizon into a haze so it was hard to tell where the sky stopped and land began. It was as if a molecular reaction occurred, fusing the land and sky together.

It was an optical illusion, of course. But with only the occasional radio chatter coming through my headset, my mind was free to roam.

A perfect day for flying, not a cloud in the sky, with radar assurance that the skies would be clear all the way to my destination.

After adjusting my four-point harness, I set the controls to autopilot.

It was just me floating above the world. No passengers.

I leveled out at ten thousand feet. My favorite altitude. I liked it because for one, it was considered by many, my grandfather included, to be the safest for individual planes of this size.

The second reason was purely personal. The view on the ground at this level still looked human. I could see highways, houses of all sizes, a small-town baseball field. A freight engine snaked its way along the miles and miles of track in what looked like slow motion.

The movement of tiny cars and trains was reminiscent of when I sat at my grandfather's feet playing with my miniature airplanes, flying them high over miniature cars and buildings.

This Phenom 100 was a small jet compared to the others owned by Skye Travels, but it was smooth, responsive, and comfortable.

What more could one want from an airplane besides smooth and responsive and comfortable? A touch of luxury. Check. Exceptional speed. Check. Lots of cargo storage. Check. My Trek off-road bicycle in a color called rage red fit easily in the storage area in the back with plenty of room left for my luggage and my golf club bag.

I typically traveled light. Nothing more than an overnight bag. But this was a longer trip.

Much longer.

It would have been a typical Wednesday morning.

Except it wasn't.

Only six months.

I could live anywhere for six months. It wasn't long enough to rent an apartment, but it was too long to live in a hotel.

Betty at the office had reserved a room for me. That was all I knew at this point. A room in someone's house.

So I had closed up my twenty-first floor Uptown Houston apartment and asked the concierge to hold my mail.

My job, flying for the prestigious Skye Travels Airline, required me to do whatever was needed. And since I was not only one of the newest hires, but also had no wife and kids, I was recruited to cover for Mike Phillips, a pilot on maternity leave.

I'd met Mike, of course, and considered him to be an admirable fellow.

Notwithstanding Mike's situation, I had to do what was needed to help out the company. That my grandfather, Noah Worthington, was the founder and owner of that company didn't give me more weight. Sometimes it actually seemed like being one of Noah's grandsons gave me more responsibility by default.

Noah had told me when I was younger, before I was even considering going to work there—not that I hadn't always known that I would—that the company was ours and we had to do whatever it took to make sure it ran smoothly. I hadn't really known what he meant by that at the time, but his words branded themselves into my brain and this particular responsibility seemed to be a perfect illustration.

Another airplane flew in front of me, not close, but just close enough for me to know it was there. Two airships passing in the sky.

One day the sky would be filled with airplanes just as the freeways were filled with cars today. Already, airplanes had autopilot. One day, probably not in my lifetime, they would be as simple to operate as cars, putting most us pilots out of jobs. I imagined that they would be made of some type of metal that, like holding two magnets with like poles close together, would repel each other, preventing the airplanes from running into each other.

Perhaps they should build cars out of that type of metal, too.

My current, not really serious, girlfriend, Charlotte, had not been happy or particularly unhappy about this semi-permanent relocation. I hadn't offered to bring her with me, our relationship wasn't like that, nor had it come up in our brief conversation two days ago. I hadn't seen or talked to her since then. That was one point of relief. I had honestly expected hysterics.

The clear sky had white puffy clouds now, probably coming from the moisture of the great lakes.

I was just thirty minutes out now.

Just a three-hour flight and my life was about to be completely different. Sometimes it took three hours to get from my apartment to the airport north of Houston. Depending on traffic.

As a pilot, travel was part of my life.

That part was nothing new. Just a part of daily life.

But moving to live in a different part of the country… that was something new and unexpected.

Only six months.

CHAPTER 3

Bailey

SITTING UPSTAIRS in my little office, I worked on a marketing plan for a client in Houston.

I'd been at it for three hours and my eyes were starting to cross.

I sat back in what was the most comfortable desk chair I had ever sat in and gazed outside. Aunt Meagan had the best of everything.

The next-door neighbor was walking his Husky, a dog named Bandit, so named because the white dog's fur had what looked like a black mask over his eyes.

The sound of an incoming airplane caught my attention. As I watched, it came close enough for me to see that this plane was a Phenom, probably a Phenom 100 from what I could see from here.

It made a sweep around the island, then went in for what I knew would be a landing.

I'd only lived here for two weeks, but I already knew the patterns and was making some of my own.

In fact, I checked my phone, it was time for me to take my midday break.

I put on my lace up hiking books and grabbed a jacket before I headed outside.

The cool air beneath the bright sunshine still surprised me. Born and bred in Houston, I was accustomed to stepping outside into uncomfortable heat and humidity in the middle of the day.

But not here. Here the sun was warm and the air cool.

I walked down what had quickly become a familiar path down the sidewalk along the shoreline towards town.

Even though it was early in the season, the streets were a little more crowded every day. There was a little sandwich shop on this side of town that I liked for lunch.

Instead of inside dining, it had a walkup window and picnic tables out front. I liked that I was almost always the only customer to sit outside at the tables. Most people got their orders to go.

"Do you want the usual?" the girl behind the counter asked. Her name was Nikki and she always had a smile.

"Yes, please."

Since there was no one behind me, I waited while the cook in the back prepared my chicken burrito.

"You going to stay through the summer?" Nikki asked.

"I don't know for sure," I said. "I still have lots to pack up before I can put the house up for sale."

"I can only imagine," she said, leaning forward with her elbows on the counter. "Your aunt came here a lot, too."

"She did?"

"Sure. It's a quick walk and all."

"It gets kinda lonely in that big house," I said, watching a big white bird swoop overhead and land near the sidewalk.

"Yeah," Nikki said, looking a little perplexed. "I guess it could." She said it like she didn't think my aunt was lonely.

"What do you mean?" I asked.

"Order up," the cook called out.

Nikki grabbed my order and bagged it.

"Here you go," she said, handing over my bag and soda. "Enjoy your lunch."

I thanked her and went to sit at one of the tables to eat.

A chipmunk darted out, stood up on his hind legs and begged.

"I'm probably not supposed to feed you," I told him, then tossed him a bite of tortilla which he grabbed and ran away with.

It was noticeably quiet without the roar of cars and other normal city sounds. It was so quiet I could hear the gentle lapping of the water against the shore.

Two boys raced past on their bicycles.

I wondered why Nikki had seemed surprised that I thought my aunt was lonely in the big house. It was a big house. It had the guest bedroom downstairs. Four bedrooms upstairs, one used as an office. The upstairs was set up so that there was even a small kitchenette. Just a refrigerator, microwave, and sink.

When I was upstairs, I felt like I was in a whole different house than downstairs. I rarely even went into the downstairs kitchen except to make morning coffee.

Nikki probably hadn't meant anything by it. Sometimes I got a little confused by the northern mid-western accent. I'm sure they were confused by my Dallas accent, too.

CHAPTER 4

Cody

WHEN I LANDED at the Mackinac runway—there was no actual airport on the island—there was a cargo wagon waiting for me.

Betty would have set that up. She had set everything up, including the room I would be living out of for the next six months.

I had all the information in my phone, but turned out I didn't need any of it. The driver already knew everything, even the address.

The sun was bright, overhead now, but away from the runway itself, it was cool in the shade of the trees.

I'd been to Mackinac Island before, but only to drop off or pick up. I had never spent any time here and had never toured anything other than what I could see from the sky.

With six months, I would have time to see everything, including the Grand Hotel and the old fort.

Betty, who knew everything about all Skye Travels activity, said an average of one flight a week out was chartered. I was going to have lots of time to explore in between charters.

Since Mike was married with one child and about to have

two, it was the perfect schedule for him, giving him lots of time for family.

I think I would go stir crazy living here.

I had to admit, though, as I climbed up on the front of the wagon, and we started down the road toward town, there was a certain charm to the island.

There were only two ways on and off the island. Boat and airplane. There was no bridge to drive over to get here. I found it fascinating that there were houses of all sizes here including the Grand Hotel. The Grand Hotel where *Somewhere in Time* had been filmed carried the distinction of having the longest porch in the world.

We traveled through downtown, an area populated with tourists, then kept going, traveling along the shoreline now.

As we left town, the only sound was the steady clip-clop of the horses' hooves and the mournful wail of the ferry's horn out on the water.

From here the lake looked like an ocean.

Outside of town, the houses along the shore as Main Street turned into Lakeshore Blvd were called cottages, but they looked more like historical Victorian and Gothic style mansions to me. The lawns were well-manicured and all had pink and yellow flowers giving them pops of color.

The driver stopped at one of those Victorian mansions, a cute house with lots of roof cuts in its three-stories. The house was a light gray, a color that matched the sky on a stormy afternoon. And my, it had windows.

"This is it," the driver said.

"Are you sure?" I asked, checking the address on my phone.

The driver laughed. "What were you expecting?"

I ran a hand along my chin and shook my hand. "I don't even know, but it wasn't this."

"Let's get you unloaded, shall we?" he asked.

"Yes." I hopped off the wagon. What had I been expecting?

Certainly not a high-rise. Maybe I had been expecting more of a cabin.

Whatever it was, I decided, it would be an adventure.

CHAPTER 5

Bailey

I **TOOK** my time getting home, walking along the shore, enjoying the soothing lapping of water against the shore. Birds gliding in the wind.

I waved at one of the neighbors out working in her front yard.

It was just so unbelievably peaceful here. When I had been a teenager, I had been too interested in friends and boys, boys mostly, to appreciate it here.

But now, ten years later, I had come a long way. I stopped and sat on one of the benches to watch a ferry as it left the docks, taking people toward the mainland.

I'd learned that there were ferries for tourists and there were boats that residents could charter to take them to the mainland for things like shopping, doctors, anything really. Once on the mainland, they could rent a car and go wherever they wanted.

The chartered boats were a lot more affordable than taking a private jet, but there were plenty of those coming and going, too.

I wondered how my aunt traveled. By ferry or boat or plane. I'd come in by ferry when I visited and the two of us didn't travel anywhere other than around the island while I was here.

There was so much I didn't know about her and yet she had left this house to me. I'd done a little research and learned that houses on Mackinac Island, like the one she left me in her will weren't easy to qualify for.

I was becoming rather attached to living here. At twenty-six, I would probably be the youngest single person living here alone, at least on purpose. I hadn't exactly done a survey, so I could be wrong. My neighbor with the Siberian husky lived alone, but he was more my aunt's age.

My extended lunch break over, I headed back to the house. I could get in a few hours of work before sunset. Watching the sun set was my next scheduled break time.

I reached the sidewalk leading to my front door—none of the houses had driveways—and turned right following the walkway.

About halfway down, surrounded by the sweet scent of magnolia blossoms, I stopped, my feet frozen to the sidewalk.

There was a man sitting on the steps of the front porch, his head down, looking at his phone. He was surrounded by three suitcases, a red bicycle, and a golf bag.

What the—?

My thoughts raced through possibilities. Another relative. Someone at the wrong house?

Then I remembered my conversation with Betty. I hadn't forgotten about it—it was too much money to forget about, but I wasn't thinking about it right now.

It had been so long, I'd actually been waiting for her to ask for her money back.

But… this could be the boarder she had sent.

She hadn't given me a name. I guess it slipped her mind.

Or maybe I hadn't answered the landline.

I started walking forward again, words of welcome on my lips.

But then he looked up.

And every cell in my body stopped functioning.

This was not possible.

But when he stood up and smiled at me, I knew who it was.

Cody Johnson was my boarder.

CHAPTER 6

Cody

AS A PILOT, I learned the art of patience early in my career. I couldn't count how many hours I had sat waiting on a client. Waiting on them to arrive at the airport. Waiting while they had a meeting. Waiting.

Sitting here watching a ferry with a tail of water behind it sail across Lake Huron was one hundred percent better than sitting in an airport terminal waiting or on an airplane or even waiting in a restaurant with a glass of seltzer water.

As far as a place to wait went, this was just about the best a man could ask for.

And I had six months to enjoy it.

I sent Betty a text letting her know I was here.

I'm here. But no one is answering the door.

BETTY

I'll give her a call.

I'll wait.

No one is answering. I've left messages, but haven't heard from her.

You paid her, right?

Yes...

Surely Betty hadn't been scammed. Not by someone who lived in a house like this.

I paid her niece. Long story.

Great. Just great.
So the niece had taken the money and run? Surely not.

I see someone coming. Maybe it's her.

Let me know.

I slipped my phone back into my jacket pocket.
She stood there in the middle of the sidewalk.
And I knew. I just knew.
The woman standing on the sidewalk looking at me.
She was Bailey Winters.
The girl who had broken my heart in college.
A day didn't pass when she didn't cross my mind in one way or another.
But I'd always pictured her the way she'd looked in college.
Hair pulled back in a high ponytail. Smiling at me with those perfectly bow shaped lips.
She'd been adorably cute.
But the grown-up version standing in front of me had shorter hair, though still long enough to fall over her shoulders. Those perfectly bow shaped lips looked like they had seen a ghost.
And she was no longer the cute college girl she had been. No. She was a beautiful young lady.
I grinned. I couldn't help it.
We had water under our bridge. Water from college.

But this was now and somehow, someway, we were here in this exact same spot at the exact same time.

There was no way that could happen by just chance alone.

No way at all.

And I would argue with anyone who dared tell me it was.

CHAPTER 7
Bailey

THE WARMTH of the sun on my head was tempered by the cool breeze coming off the lake. The last ferry of the day blew its horn indicating it was time for those wanting to leave today to make their way to the dock.

The magnolia trees my aunt had planted, one on either side of her sidewalk, filled the air with their springtime blossoms.

I unconsciously swept my tousled hair out of my face as I blinked in disbelief. How many times had my heart stumbled when I thought I saw Cody across a crowded room?

It wouldn't be him though. It never was.

He was from Houston and as far as I could tell—which was not at all—he still lived there. I had looked for him on social media, but it was like he had ceased to exist. Not a good feeling.

While he was from Houston, I was from Dallas.

We had met up for two years at Texas A & M. It was supposed to have lasted forever, but like most college romances, it didn't.

Cody Johnson had been handsome when we were in college. The handsome aviation instructor who swaggered around campus wearing his dark aviator shades. I had been the one to catch his eye, but I never really trusted it.

Cody Johnson could have any girl he wanted and I always knew that he would be leaving before long. That he stayed in College Station for the two years he did after graduation was surprising.

Time had been kind to him. Like many men, he had gotten even more handsome over the years.

He would be thirty-one now. I kept track of his birthday. February 20. Every year on his birthday, my heart would break a little bit more, knowing that another year had passed without him.

It didn't help one bit that it was my fault we had broken up.

When he smiled at me, I was no longer a twenty-six-year-old woman on Mackinac Island. I was an eighteen-year-old college freshman at Texas A & M.

How many times had I imagined this moment? I had imagined it in a hundred different ways.

But never like this.

Never, not once, in the six years we had been apart had I imagined finding him waiting for me on the steps of my aunt's house on Mackinac Island.

"How? Why?" I don't even know if the words were coming out of my mouth or if they were only in my head.

While I stood, my feet frozen to the sidewalk, he stood up and closed the distance separating us.

Without a word, he swept me up into his arms, off my feet, and twirled me around.

A happier greeting I had not imagined.

My imagination had rarely gotten past merely seeing him again.

That was about as far as my brain would let me go with those particular fantasies.

Probably a protective mechanism to keep me from falling apart.

Before I could even catch my breath, he set me on my feet and just looked at me.

His eyes locked onto mine and I knew I didn't stand a chance.

His eyes were so very blue. Blue like a deep blue sky, they mesmerized me.

"You're here," I murmured, my voice barely audible.

He ran a hand along the slope of my cheek. "And you," he said simply.

"How?"

"I've heard it said that Mackinac Island has a kind of magic."

His words sent a shiver along my spine. I'd heard that as well. I thought it was the water of the lake sweeping against the sandy shore. The mournful cry of the ferry as it came and went, taking people to and from this island that seemed to be stuck in time where cars weren't allowed. Where people traveled by horse and buggy instead of fancy cars.

That, I'd thought, was the magic.

But if Cody was here, then the magic was something else.

I nodded, unable to think of any words to convey the overwhelming feelings consuming me at this particular moment.

Cody, however, did not seem to be equally affected.

He broke eye contact and swept a hand in the general direction of the porch.

"I don't know why you're here," he said. "but I think I'm supposed to live here for the next six months."

"Oh." Everything fell into place like those last pieces of a puzzle that tied everything together.

He was the one. Betty from Houston had called, what was it, two weeks ago, and reserved a room for... someone.

Who would have thought that someone would be Cody Johnson, my college sweetheart?

"Why are you here?" he asked.

The last time I had seen him was in College Station. We had stood outside the parking lot of our favorite Mexican restaurant when we had said goodbye. Seven years ago.

And he was acting like this was just another Wednesday afternoon.

"I 'um live here."

"No," he shook his head, frowning at me in disbelief.

"Yes," I nodded. "I own this house."

I don't know why it seemed important that he know that.

"Your aunt?" he asked, though I wasn't sure how I would know that.

"She left it to me." The matter-of-fact words seemed to bring me a bit out of my daze.

He looked at me with what had to be about a million questions.

I just shrugged and keyed in the code to the door.

I held the door open as he brought in his three suitcases, then his bag of golf clubs.

"You look like you're moving in," I said.

"I kinda think I am. At least for a while. Is there some place I can stash my bicycle?"

"In the back," I said. "There's no garage, but there's a storage room that locks."

"Huh," he said. "No garage."

"Why would there be?"

"I'm not sure. For buggies, maybe."

I smiled then for the first time since I'd seen him sitting on the steps of the porch.

"Yes," I said, biting my lip to keep from laughing out loud. "maybe for buggies."

As he walked his bicycle around back, I closed the door and stood there grinning like a fool. Seeing him… having him here… was so surreal, it broke something loose inside of me. Or maybe it wasn't loose so much as it was the pieces of my heart shifting back into place.

Whatever it was, I needed to catch my breath.

I sat on the sofa and stared at the painting of the unknown couple on the wall.

I wondered if Aunt Meagan knew who the couple was. Since she had left their painting on the wall, it seemed likely that she did. Or maybe she had just liked it because it was old and seemed to go with the house.

It hadn't occurred to me to ask her when I was a teen.

And now that she was gone, I couldn't ask her.

I was just about to take the picture down off the wall and look to see if anything was written on the back when Cody came in through the back door.

"You forgot to lock the door?" he asked.

"Maybe," I said. "I check it at night."

He just looked at me, hands on his hips, as though he didn't know who I was.

"Is that my room back there?" he asked.

"Right," I said. "It is."

"Do you need some help?"

"Nah," he said. "Maybe a glass of water if you have it."

I went into the kitchen and, after filling a glass with tap water, I pressed my hands against the counter in an effort to stop them from trembling.

Cody Johnson.

Right here on Mackinac Island.

Things could not possibly be more surreal.

CHAPTER 8

Cody

AFTER I PARKED my bicycle inside the currently unlocked storage shed and went in through the back, unlocked door, I found Bailey sitting on the sofa staring at an old painting hanging on the wall.

After she went off to get me a glass of water, I rolled my luggage into the guest room that would be mine for the next six months.

It was a decent sized room. Not much smaller than the bedroom in my high-rise condo.

It had an oversized four-poster bed with a white comforter and pillow shams. They matched the wispy white curtains that were more for decoration than for function.

In my condo, I had a button that I could push to lower and raise my blinds. I walked to the one window. No blinds.

People on Mackinac Island must be trusting by nature.

I didn't trust them. There were too many unknowns, mostly tourists. I would bet money that not all those tourists came over just for sightseeing.

But I was fresh out of Houston so I kept my opinions to myself, for the moment at least.

Not one to waste time, I began to unpack my suitcases,

hanging things on the hangers on the rod in the armoire and putting other items on the shelves, since there was no closet. It must have been bigger than it looked because everything fit inside, including my shoes.

I nested my three suitcases and stood them on one side of the armoire.

Bailey stood at the door, holding a glass of water.

"Thank you," I said, drinking deeply.

"Did you come in on the Phenom?" she asked.

"Yes," I said. "Did you see me?"

"Maybe," she said, turning away with a little shrug.

I grinned. "You remember what I taught you about airplanes?"

The thought that she remembered those things from so many years ago made me feel warm and gooey inside. I hadn't even known whether she was paying attention at the time.

"How could I not?" she asked, tilting her head to the side. "You didn't talk about much other than airplanes. And flying. And aviation."

"It was my thing." Is my thing.

I tried to remember what her major had been in college, then after taxing my brain on it, I remembered that she had been in general studies her first two years, when I had known her.

"Did you ever settle on a major?" I asked, remembering some of ones she had toyed with. "Psychology? History? Education?"

"Marketing," she said.

"Marketing. I don't think that was one you were considering."

"I'm impressed that you remember."

I nodded. "Then we're even."

She turned and I followed her back to the kitchen. I went to the sink and refilled my water.

"The water tastes good," she said. "They do some kind of filtering thing to it."

"Huh. How long have you lived here?"

"About two weeks."

Just two weeks.

"I'm really sorry about your aunt."

"Me too," she said. "She was a good person."

"Did you know?" I asked, trying to figure out how to ask delicately. "Did you know all this was going to be yours someday?"

"Not in the least."

"It must have been quite the surprise."

"Everything about Mackinac Island is turning out to be a surprise," she said.

I grinned again and she smiled, despite obviously trying not to.

"Of all the gin joints," I said.

"Gin joints?"

"Casablanca," I said. "Remember? We watched it together."

"There were so many."

How could she forget a line like that in a moment like this?

"Marketing suits you," I said, changing the subject again. "Do you… work here while you're on the island?"

"Yes. I'm working on a project right now," she said. "for a company in Dallas." She added when I didn't say anything.

I nodded again and would have said something about the global economy, but this seemed neither the place or the time to talk politics to Bailey.

This was the time to find out more about her personal life.

"You're here alone?" I asked, glancing down at her finger. I'd always operated on the philosophy that if there wasn't a ring on it, the girl was fair game. All's fair in love and war, someone famous said.

"Yes," she said.

Something was different. The Bailey I knew could talk circles around me. But this Bailey was quiet and complicated.

Traits I had trouble reconciling with what I already knew about her.

Things I knew from the college student Bailey. It was going to take me a few minutes to adjust to the new her, especially missing large chunk of years.

We couldn't just pick up where we left off. Could we?

Bailey was the one unresolved relationship in my head.

The one I let go that I sincerely regretting.

But it hadn't been my fault.

Of all the gin joints.

CHAPTER 9
Bailey

AFTER GETTING CODY SETTLED IN—IT didn't take long—he mostly settled himself in, I went back upstairs to my office and sat at my desk.

I didn't *work* at my office. I just *sat* at my desk.

How was I supposed to work when the one man I never stopped loving had just walked back into my life?

I was staring at my computer screen when I saw the light curtains fluttering at my window out of the corner of my eye. The window was closed, so it wasn't from the breeze.

Watching the curtains closely for a moment, waiting for them to move again, but they didn't, I got up and went to stand at the window.

Just as I did, I saw Cody riding his bright red bicycle out from around the corner of the house, down the sidewalk and out to the road. He turned right instead of left toward town.

I ran a hand along the soft cotton curtain, looking for some reason why it would have fluttered. I had seen the curtain flutter.

After Cody disappeared around the bend into the trees, I sat back down at my desk and stared out at the horizon.

It was almost that time of day when I usually stopped work,

poured a glass of wine, and went out to watch the sunset over the water.

But today I had only worked half a day.

Since staring at my computer screen did not count as work, I would just come back and work through the evening.

I tapped the edge of my computer, then gave up and closed the lid. I wasn't going to be getting any work done today.

I wandered downstairs and sat on the sofa where I studied the old painting of the couple on the wall in front of me.

Again, I wondered who they were and why my aunt had left the painting there.

Her décor was more modern. In fact, this was the only item I'd come across that seemed to be an artifact.

My thoughts wound themselves back to Cody.

Cody Johnson.

I still couldn't wrap my brain around how it was that he came to be here.

Of all the places—or all the gin joints as Cody said—how had we met up here?

This was in no way near College Station or Houston or Dallas. Any one of those places, coming in each other's orbit again would have seemed at least plausible.

But here...

My aunt just happened to have bought a house on Mackinac Island and just happened to leave it to me. Cody just happened to be sent here by work to this island... to this house...

Where I just happened to be.

It wasn't the least bit plausible.

Sometimes, like now, I struggled to remember why I had broken up with him.

It wasn't because I hadn't loved him. I did.

It was because... I had been afraid. I hadn't known that at the time.

But over the years, I had figured it out.

I was the one who had stopped answering my phone.

CHAPTER 10

Cody

I STOPPED on the far side of the island and walked along the water's edge.

The quietness was deafening. It was almost like I was the only person on the island. On my own deserted island.

And, God help me, the girl I'd never stopped loving was on this island, too.

But she didn't know. She didn't know a day hadn't passed when I hadn't thought about her. I still didn't understand why she hadn't wanted to wait for me.

I had asked her to.

I had told her that I would only be gone for one year, maybe two. By then she would have graduated and she could have joined me.

But she'd said no. Not in words. She hadn't said no in words. But I had seen it in her eyes.

And then when she didn't answer phone… my worst fears were confirmed.

Eventually I stopped calling.

Within the year, I was living in Houston and working for Skye Travels. It would have been no problem to find her. I could have flown up to College Station and showed up at her house.

I actually had flown up there one time. I'd sat in the plane for an hour before I had simply turned around and flown back to Houston.

I loved her too much to push her. If she had a reason for not wanting to talk to me, I had to respect that.

Besides, there were things I hadn't told her. I hadn't told her that I was Noah Worthington's grandson. Noah Worthington, founder and owner of Skye Travels.

She had never gone home with me and I had never gone home with her.

I figured we'd meet each other's parents eventually. But I had been too laissez-faire. As much as I hated to admit it, I had taken her for granted.

I'd thought she would be there when I wanted her.

That had not worked too well for me. She had probably figured it out.

So I had moved on. I dated, but I always held a part of myself back in my relationships.

No one compared to Bailey. No one even came close.

I'd heard my Grandma Savannah compare me to her only son, Uncle Quinn. I hadn't understood that.

But I did know that Uncle Quinn had looked for Aunt Noelle for years after he had lost touch with her. He didn't so much as even date anyone else during those years.

He was a stronger man than I.

I could see where Grandma Savannah would see a resemblance between the two of us.

The difference was I knew where to find Bailey, at least at first. And yet I had let her go.

Over the years, after she would have left College Station, I had searched for her, but it was almost as if she had disappeared off the face of the earth. I hoped she was happy.

I really wanted her to be happy even if she couldn't be with me.

I cared that much for her.

But now, somehow, someway, fate had intervened to give us a second chance.

Something like this could not happen by accident. I was certain of that.

The country was too big. I had not even known she had an aunt, much less an aunt on Mackinac Island.

And yet, here we were.

In the same place at the same time.

I watched as the sun splashed an array of color across the sky as it started its downward trek over the horizon.

It was stunningly beautiful here.

A boat sailed along, too far out for me to do more than catch a glimpse and too far out to even hear its motor.

There was just the gentle lapping of the water against the shore. The water was cold. Too cold to swim in, but it looked inviting, the way the sun glinted off the surface.

I picked up a rock and tossed it out into the water, watching the ripples.

This was something I had never expected. I had never expected to have a second chance with her. Maybe this time I would do things differently.

I had learned a few things since then.

The most important thing I had learned was to never, never take the girl you love for granted or to even give her the chance to think you took her for granted even if you didn't.

Picking up another rock, I tossed it from one hand to the other.

This seemed to me like a crossroads.

I could play it cool and see what happened—sort of what I had done in College Station—and look where that had gotten me. Or I could go about the whole thing completely different.

I could put myself out there and take a chance by going out on a limb with everything I had.

The way I saw it, there was no middle ground. Not this time.

The middle ground would put us right back where we had been all those years before.

I tossed the stone out into the water.

This was where I decided what I wanted to do.

And the one thing I did know was that this time I didn't want to risk letting her slip out of my fingers again.

CHAPTER 11
Bailey

AFTER GIVING up on getting any work done and not having a clue when Cody would be back, not that it mattered—he was a grown man and we weren't dating anymore, I opened a bottle of chardonnay, poured some into one of Aunt Meagan's wine glasses—my wine glasses now—and took it outside to sit on my second-floor balcony with an unobstructed view of the lake.

The sun splashed an array of colors across the sky as it dipped over the horizon. The scent of magnolias and daffodils filled the air along with the occasional hint of food from downtown.

My stomach grumbled a bit, but I had taught myself to eat only once a day, most days. Intermittent fasting.

The wine probably cancelled out the fasting, but I figured I was doing better than most people.

I watched as white birds floated along, dipping into the water for their prey. A deer came up to the edge of the water, her two spotted fawns following along behind her.

So peaceful. Then the neighbor next door brought his dog, Bandit out for his evening frolic.

The mother deer twitched her ears and took off running, her

babies behind her before Bandit even had a sense that they were nearby.

Bandit ran down the sidewalk, then turned and ran back.

The neighbor, seeing me as he passed, lifted a hand in greeting.

I waved back and wondered.

I wondered if he and my aunt were friends.

Maybe she wasn't reclusive just because she lived here on the island.

There were a lot of things I didn't know and assumptions I had made that were probably off course.

I heard Cody's bicycle heading back before I even saw him.

I needed to decided what I was going to do about Cody.

One option was to pack up and leave as I had originally planned. Pretend that I was unaffected.

Another option was to not let him change what I was doing. Basically just pretend he wasn't here.

I had already ruled out the first two.

Beyond that, I wasn't sure what I was going to do.

For one thing, since I had been the one to stop answering the phone, I wasn't sure how he was going to react to me.

After turning onto the sidewalk, he hopped off his bicycle and unstrapped a couple of bags from the back before he headed to the front door.

A few feet this way, he looked up and saw me. Stopping, he grinned.

"Hi," he said.

"Hi," I said, straightening in my chair and putting a hand over my eyes to shield my view from the sun so I could see him better.

"Can you come down?" he asked.

"Why?" But my lips quivered on the edge of a smile. He looked so charmingly boyish.

He held up the two bags.

"I brought dinner," he said.

"Oh." This was not what I had been expecting. Not in the least. "I'll be right down."

What was a girl supposed to do when a guy brought dinner? She had no choice, but to join him. It was quite simply the polite thing to do.

CHAPTER 12

Cody

I COULD CLAIM I had a good memory. It wasn't a stretch. As a pilot, I remembered all sorts of codes and formulas and all the other things that came with being a pilot.

If you'd asked me how Charlotte, the girl I'd taken to lunch and dinner a dozen times and quite recently, too, took her hamburger, I couldn't remember. Didn't see that I had cause to. She ordered for herself and I rarely paid attention.

But I remembered that Bailey liked her hamburgers well-done, extra tomato, pickles, and onions. No mustard. And she used hamburgers as an excuse to eat French fries.

It was just one of those things that I remembered. I might not have been the best boyfriend, but I remembered things about Bailey. And, yes, I remembered these things from six years ago.

By the time I unpacked the paper bags onto the breakfast table in the kitchen, Bailey was coming down the stairs.

She looked cute in her jeans and gray sweatshirt with Texas A & M splashed across the front. It sent a stutter through my heart, seeing her dressed like a college student like this.

But like earlier in the day, she wore her hair loose around her shoulders. Her eyes met mine and she smiled.

"You brought French fries," she said happily.

It was such a little thing, but I felt like she had just given me the highest praise possible, making me feel like I'd just earned first place in something. I tried not to puff out my chest.

"Milady," I said, sliding out one of the chairs, sweeping an arm to indicate she should sit.

"Thank you," she said. I didn't miss the little flush of color that swept across her cheeks.

"Do you want a plate?" I asked. "Or is this okay?"

"This is fine," she said, unwrapping her hamburger and taking a peek under the bun.

She looked up at me with a perplexed expression as she took the lid off one of the ketchup cups. Another thing I remembered, she likes lots of ketchup.

"Everything good?" I asked, sitting down next to her.

"It's perfect," she said.

I smiled to myself.

Tactic one in place. Let her know I remember the little things about her.

"Good choice," she said after tasting her burger.

"You've eaten at this place then?" I asked. "The Mustang Lounge."

"No," she said. "It's on the other side of town." She smiled. "But I will now."

The other side of town.

It was about thirty minutes from here on foot. I guess it was all about perspective.

"I wonder why Betty from Houston never called me back to give me your name and arrival date," she said, dipping a French fry into the ketchup.

I looked blankly at her a moment.

"But she did. She said she left messages. She even called when I got here." I shrugged. "But you weren't home."

"She must have called the landline."

"Probably," I said. "There's no answering machine?"

"I thought there was," she said, looking around the kitchen as though she might have misplaced the phone.

I spotted what looked like an old phone from the last century—1930s maybe—over on the counter. It looked like a rotary phone, but the handset was obviously cordless. "Is that it?"

Bailey dabbed another French fry into ketchup and looked over her shoulder.

"Yes," she said. "It has a horrible ring."

I shoved my chair back and, picking up the cordless handset, tried to hide my smile. "I see the problem," I said.

"Yeah? What's wrong with it?"

I placed the handset on the phone's cradle.

"It needs to be charged," I said. "And… it's got an answering machine, but it's unplugged."

"Oh. I 'um."

"It's okay." After I plugged it back into the outlet, I went to my chair and started eating again.

"How do you know about old phones like that?"

"I guess I grew up around a lot of old people that still like to hold onto an actual phone."

She looked at me like I had three heads.

"The receiver," I said. "They like holding a receiver." I imitated holding the phone up to my ear.

She nodded. "I understand that. I guess I just didn't realize the handset wasn't on the charger."

"And how would you know that, right?"

"Actually. I think we had those when I was little girl."

I could just see her as a little girl. I bet her favorite color was pink.

"I think I had a pink phone in my room," she said. "Before I got an iPhone when I turned seventeen."

I busted out laughing. I couldn't help it.

Her brow furrowed, she just looked blankly at me, obviously not understanding my humor.

And I laughed even more.

CHAPTER 13

Bailey

I **BIT** my lip to keep from joining Cody in his laughter.

"You shouldn't be laughing at my expense," I said.

"You do know I'm laughing with you, not at you."

"If you say so," I said, feigning offense.

The phone on the counter chimed.

"You can laugh if you want to, but I did not unplug the phone and..." I held up a finger for emphasis. "I am certain I knew to put the phone back on the charger."

He laughed again.

"Want to bet?" he asked. "I bet there are messages from Betty on there."

"I bet there are, too. But..."

He shrugged and went back to eating.

I got up and pressed play.

You have six new messages.

I frowned at Cody over my shoulder.

There was one from someone I didn't know asking about Aunt Meagan. And the other five were from Betty from Houston. She gave me Cody's name and arrival date. Even called earlier today to try to find out if I was home to let him in.

"I don't understand," I said. "If it was unplugged, how did it take a message?"

"I don't know," he said, unconcerned. "Do you have a cat?"

"No. I don't have a cat. And even if I did, I'm not sure it could unplug something from the wall."

"We'll figure it out," he said. "Finish eating."

"I'm finished," I said, but I sat down anyway and started wrapping everything up.

"Don't throw out the fries," he said, sliding them in his direction.

Putting my elbows on the table, I watched him eat. He'd always had a good appetite.

"How did you end up here?" I asked. "Really?"

"Skye Travels keeps a small jet here on the island. The pilot, his name is Mike, who lives here, is taking six months off for maternity leave."

"Maternity leave."

"He and his wife are having their second baby."

"I see. They live on the island?" I don't know why, but I had somehow imagined that young people wouldn't live here on purpose.

I suppose I thought that because it was so isolated and there were no malls, no cultural events, limited restaurants.

But maybe I was wrong.

"Are they, Mike and his wife, from here?" I asked, trying to align this new information with my perspective or maybe realign my perspective with the new information.

"No," he said. "Mike is from… Dallas maybe. I'm not sure. He's moved around a lot."

"What about his wife?"

"A small town, maybe, in the Midwest. I'm not sure. But you'd like them."

"I'm sure," I said, but I felt a little better. If Mike's wife was from a small town, then she would be used to living in an area without malls and cultural events, and lots of restaurants. This wouldn't be a stretch for her.

"It's a beautiful night out," he said. "with a clear forecast."

I smiled at his mention of the forecast. Pilots were amateur meteorologists. I'd always found it cute how he pored over his iPad, double checking the official weather reports. He wouldn't leave the ground without computing his own forecast.

"The weather is interesting," I said. "even on a rainy day."

He smiled. "But no rain tonight. Do you want to go for a walk along the shore?"

My heart stuttered.

He was asking me to go on a romantic walk along the shore in the moonlight.

Even when we had known each other back in college, I couldn't remember any moonlight strolls.

Maybe a moonlight flight in a Cessna, but not a moonlight stroll.

"Okay," I said. "I'll take a walk with you."

I still hadn't wrapped my head around him being here to begin with and now he was looking at me with those blue eyes that reminded me of a clear summer sky or one of those tiny blue daisies that sprouted up on the lawn to announce spring every year.

I was probably being dramatic, but I couldn't help feeling that taking a moonlight stroll with Cody Johnson could very well be a life-changing event.

CHAPTER 14

Cody

BETWEEN THE MOONLIGHT reflecting off the lake and the steady movement of the lighthouse beacon, there was plenty of light to guide our way.

As we approached town, little lamp posts lit our way.

It was a bit surreal walking along the sidewalk on Mackinac Island, in the moonlight, with Bailey.

I'd messed things up with her last time. I wasn't going to do it again.

I was going to court her like I had never courted a woman before.

"It's beautiful here, isn't it?" she asked as we neared the town.

She'd tied her hair back, but a strand had pulled loose and fluttered across her face.

"More beautiful than I ever would have expected," I said, watching her, and talking about her, not the view.

It was beautiful here, but it didn't matter to me where we were.

I was just happy to be with her.

Something in the universe had shifted and brought us back together.

I didn't know that it was just one thing. Maybe it was a lot of things.

As I thought about it, I decided that a lot of things had to fall into place for us to land right here right now.

Mike had to be having a baby. Bailey's aunt had to leave the house to her. Bailey's Aunt Meagan and Betty, the office manager of Skye Travels, had to be friends. What were the odds of all those things happening?

We walked over a little wooden bridge, nothing but a trickle of water beneath.

"I saw an ice cream shop when I rode through town earlier. Do you want to get some ice cream?" I asked.

She looked at me sideways and tucked that loose strand of hair behind an ear.

"Okay," she said.

There were more people in town than I had expected. If I thought about it at all, I'd have thought everyone left the island at night.

"There are people still here," I said.

"They have a lot of hotels," she said. "And bed and breakfasts."

"Huh."

Music spilled out of a bar as we neared. Seems Mackinac Island had a nightlight, too.

As a group of guys spilled out of one of the bars, I took Bailey's hand and guided her through the people.

Her hand felt good in mine. New and familiar at the same time. It was a rather odd sensation. I'd wondered what it would be like, holding her hand again after all these years.

It was sort of like going home again.

I had been young and dumb. That was the only explanation I had.

We reached the ice cream parlor and got in line with the teenagers.

"I think we're the oldest ones here," I leaned over to whisper in her ear.

She smelled like lavender and vanilla and sent all sorts of delicious tingles through me.

"We weren't much older than they are," she said. "when we last had ice cream."

"Did we have ice cream?" I asked. I blamed my memory lapse on the lavender and vanilla. I hadn't forgotten too many details about her.

"A couple of times," she said. "but it was just on campus. Nothing like this."

"Right." That sounded about right. That was before I knew what I had in her.

We got to the counter.

"What would you like?" the teenage boy behind the counter wearing a white hat shaped like an upside down boat asked.

I looked down at Bailey. "Three scoops. One vanilla. One chocolate. And one cookie dough."

"How do you remember that?" she asked, looking at me with something akin to awe.

"Is that what you still like?" I asked.

"Yes," she said. "But you remembered?"

I squeezed her hand, then relayed our order to the teen and we stepped aside to wait.

"I remember everything about you, Chère." I said, leaning close enough that she could feel my breath on her skin.

And the more I remembered, the more I wanted to know. So far I was getting everything right. And yet... I knew there would be things about her I didn't know. Things related only to the grown-up version of Bailey.

Those were things I couldn't wait to learn.

And yet, I also loved already knowing things about her. Things that hadn't changed with time.

It made me wonder. Would kissing her be the same? Or would it be different?

CHAPTER 15

Bailey

CODY and I sat on a bench and watched the tourists walk up and down the street.

Older people walking hand in hand. Young people, laughing as they walked by. A lot of couples.

Now I knew. Now I knew what it was like to be with a boyfriend and eat ice cream instead of just watching other people, other couples like I had done when I was a teen.

Except that Cody and I weren't a couple.

It was kinda weird. Because we had been before, it seemed like we should be.

Cody and I had been together for two years. It was the longest relationship I'd ever had before or since.

And now I wondered about him. He could have a girlfriend. He wasn't wearing a ring. And if he was married I didn't think he would be here having ice cream and taking moonlight strolls with me.

I remembered that Cody liked rocky road ice cream, but he was always mixing up his other two scoops. Tonight he'd gotten one scoop of chocolate and one of vanilla to go with his rocky road. It was a lot less adventurous tonight than what he used to get. I'd remembered he sometimes got pistachio or caramel or butter pecan.

I wondered if he had settled into getting the same thing or if he still mixed things up.

"Taste this," he said, holding out a spoonful of ice cream from his cup.

"It's rocky road," I said, wrinkling my nose.

"With a swirl of vanilla and chocolate. Try it."

I leaned in and slipped the ice cream he offered into my mouth.

"What do you think?" he asked. "It's not so bad mixed like that."

"You're right," I said. "It's okay."

He just grinned and took another bite.

I couldn't get past the intimacy of eating off his spoon.

I'd always equated eating after someone with kissing them. I only ate after people I would kiss.

And that sent my thoughts down a whole off-limits path.

"Did you know that Mackinac had a nightlife?" he asked.

"I knew something about it," I said.

"Huh." He watched people walk past us, not even seeing us. We simply blended into their background just as they blended into ours.

"What have you been up to?" I asked, keeping my tone purposely light.

It was a heavy question that I wanted to ask and at the same time didn't want to know the answer to.

"Working mostly," he said.

"Skye Travels."

"Yes."

I waited for him to expand on his answer, but he didn't.

"Have you worked for them long?"

"I've worked for them the whole time."

"What about your other thing?" I couldn't remember exactly what it had been. Something that was supposed to give him more experience, more flight hours and training. What I did remember was that it was in Alabama. Back then that had seemed like a world away from College Station.

"I didn't do that very long."

"Huh," I said, just as he had said earlier.

I wanted to blame him for not telling me that he was back in Texas. And yet I couldn't do that.

I was the one who had stopped answering his calls.

Water under the bridge.

CHAPTER 16

Cody

MUSIC SPILLED from the bar across the street and a restaurant two doors down, mixing together to form a unique sound. One that mixed with conversations swirling all around us. The steady clip clop of horses and buggies passed, but most people walked.

Main Street was lit up with street lights.

I quickly learned that I didn't know as much as about courting a lady as I had thought.

I had to balance a line between coming on too fast and creepy and being charming and persistent.

The charming part wasn't so hard. The persistent part was a little bit more challenging. Not because I wasn't feeling persistent. But because I was out of practice.

Had I ever been persistent?

I'd let women wander in and out of my life without any kind of commitment.

I didn't want to think too hard about what that said about me.

My older brother Benjamin had been far worse than I was. He'd had a girl in every port until he met Chloé.

Benjamin had fallen in love with Chloé at first sight and his days of being a playboy had been over just like that.

I wasn't a playboy. I was faithful to whoever I was dating. I'd been faithful to Charlotte.

It was just I hadn't really *cared* about her.

When I didn't hear from her for the two days before I moved up here, I was actually relieved.

Did that mean we were broken up?

I hadn't really known until I'd seen Bailey.

Now I knew. Charlotte and I were definitely broken up.

As I finished off my ice cream, it occurred to me that I should probably tell Charlotte.

Maybe I'd send her a text.

She probably didn't care one way or the other either.

That was how we had stayed together for as long as we had.

I was like my brother, Benjamin, though, in that I had found the woman I loved and my party days were over. Just like that.

Did it count that she and I had dated in college? For two years?

I decided it did. And I decided it made things even better.

We could zip through the part of trying to figure out if we liked each other. Learning the basics, like what kind of things we liked to do and what kinds of things we liked to eat.

And yet there were things we didn't know. Things to learn about each other.

It was the best of both worlds.

"Are you finished with that?" I asked, noticing that Bailey had set her ice cream on the bench next to her. she'd only eaten about one third of it.

"Yeah. Do you want it?"

Maybe. "No, but I'll toss it for you."

She handed me her empty bowl and I tossed it in the can two feet from our bench. It was such a little thing, but I liked doing it for her.

This was one of those things that I wanted to get into this time around.

I wanted to do things for her. I wanted to be her person. To take care of her.

Even here, tonight, I didn't want to let her out of my sight.

It was crazy. She was a grown woman and I was sure she could take care of herself, but that was the thing.

I *wanted* to take care of her.

When I'd driven to the airport this morning and flown up to Mackinac Island, I'd had no idea that my life was about to change.

Now all I had to do was to convince her that she and I were meant to be together.

If she was still mad at me from six years ago, then that could be a problem.

Fortunately, although she didn't seem to be mad at me, she did seem to be a little bit distant.

I had to give her time.

And I had to remember that she hadn't expected to see me today either.

CHAPTER 17

Bailey

CODY and I walked along the sidewalk next to the water, hand in hand.

He'd taken my hand when we had walked through the crowds in town and now it had just become natural.

It was like those six years we'd been apart simply vanished.

We walked slowly, as though we were reluctant to get back to the house.

Like we were on a normal date.

But when we got home, it wasn't like we weren't going to see each other in the morning.

He wasn't going to just drop me off at my door and go his own way.

He was my boarder.

I'd been paid good money for him to stay in what was now my own house.

If I had known Cody was the one who would be staying with me, I was pretty sure I would not have charged him.

Of course, he wasn't the one who had paid. It had been the company he worked for. Skye Travels.

Somehow that seemed to justify things in my head.

An owl greeted us as we neared the house about the same

time that clouds passed over the moon, making it harder to see where we were going.

"It's like being in the country," he said.

"It is the country," I said, with a little laugh.

And that, I realized was the thing that surprised me about liking it here on the island.

It was like living in a very small town. A very small town with lots of tourists, but still a very small town. And out here, along the shoreline, there were neighbors, but they were very limited.

I hadn't officially met any of my neighbors yet. I only knew the one to the right because I saw him outside walking his dog.

I'd never considered myself to be someone who would like living in the country.

I'd sort of been rethinking that already, but now, walking along the shore hand in hand with Cody, I realized I had to be careful.

If I wasn't careful, he was going to steal my heart... again... and then what would happen after six months? Or maybe less than six months. I hadn't decided how long I was going to stay here.

Our roles had flipped. I needed to get back to Dallas. I still had an apartment there, even if all my work was done from wherever I was with my computer.

And yet... I wasn't in any hurry.

I wasn't even sure I wanted to go back there.

But if I stayed here. To be with him. And then he left. I'd be back where I was six years ago.

We made it to my sidewalk and headed to the front door.

"We're home," I said. "You left your bicycle out."

"I'll take it around," he said. "and meet you inside."

"Okay," I said.

Damn it. When he let go of my hand, I already missed him.

This was not a good sign for me. Missing him when he was

just going around back to put his bicycle in the locked storage room.

I let myself in and locked the door behind me.

I dropped my purse on the table next to the door and, taking my cell phone with me, went into the kitchen.

The landline sat there, just like it was supposed to. Plugged in and charging. I hadn't unplugged it. I was certain of that. Why would I?

Apparently Aunt Meagan had used the landline as her business line. I hadn't answered any personal calls on it.

I wandered from there to the main living area with the little sofa and the painting on the wall of what I had come to think of as the newlyweds.

I was still studying them, contemplating who they might be, when Cody came in through the back door.

He came over and stood next to me.

"Who are they?" he asked.

"I don't have a clue."

"Your aunt must have known them," he said.

I turned and looked into his eyes.

"I thought the same thing."

Then I reached up to pull the painting off the wall.

CHAPTER 18

Cody

"IT'S STUCK," Bailey said, tugging at the old painting of a couple on the wall.

She had both hands up, one on either side of the painting.

"Want some help?" I asked.

"No," she said. "I should... Be. Able. To.... Work. It... Loose."

She might think she could work it loose, but it looked to me like it was stuck pretty tightly. Maybe someone had stuck it on the wall while the paint was still wet or maybe it had been up on the wall for just too long.

I went up behind her and reached up to help her work the frame loose.

The painting suddenly came loose in her hands and she fell back against me, into my arms.

"Whoa," I said, steadying her on her feet to keep her from falling. "I think you got it."

"It was stuck," she said.

She smelled like vanilla and lavender and she was soft in my arms. I wrapped my arms around her waist, pulling her against me for just a minute as she found her footing.

"I've got it now," she said. "Thank you."

I released her, but stayed close enough to make sure she was steady. She took the painting to the breakfast room and laid it on the table face down.

"Should we take the back off?" she asked, running a hand over the cardboard.

"It's the only way to find out if there's anything under there."

She picked at one of the metal clasps with her fingernail.

"Wait," I said, going to the silverware drawer and coming back with a butter knife.

One by one, I bent the metal clasps up.

"Ready?" I asked.

"Let's do it."

Moving carefully, I lifted the cardboard and set it aside.

"It's a letter," she said with a glance up at me.

The folded piece of paper had the name *Carlton* written on it.

She picked it up and unfolded it, the brittle paper crinkling in her hands. I read over her shoulder as she read out loud.

My dearest Carlton,

They tell me you were lost at sea.

But I want you to know that I will never give up on you.

If there is the remotest chance that you could still be out there somewhere, I will wait for you.

Know that I will stay here at this house. Until the end of time. And I will wait for you.

I will wait because true love never dims.

Your truest love,

Amelia

She turned and met my gaze, searching.

Her eyes were green, like the dark green of Kentucky bluegrass.

I swallowed and forced myself to focus on something other than her eyes… her lips…

The letter would be a good thing to focus on.

"That must be Amelia and Carlton," I said, glancing down at the letter to make sure I had their names right.

Dropping into the nearest chair, she reread the letter. I sat in the chair next to her and waited.

"Does this mean he never got this letter?" she asked, looking back at me.

"I guess it's possible," I said. "But someone had to put it in this frame."

"We should put it back," she said, suddenly, with a quick glance over her shoulder.

"Why?" I asked.

"I don't know. It just feels like we invaded their privacy.

I didn't want to be the one to remind her, but Amelia and Carlton weren't in a place to have any privacy.

"This letter was written in 1811," I pointed out, unable not to say something.

"How do you know?"

"It's written on the back."

She turned the paper over and blew out a breath. Then she carefully refolded the paper and placed it back where we found it.

I placed the cardboard back over it and one by one pressed the little metal clasps back down.

"We have to put it back on the wall," she said, very seriously.

"I'll do it," I said, trying to ignore the little shiver that ran down my spine.

CHAPTER 19

Bailey

AFTER CODY LIT a fire in the fireplace (gas), we sat on the floor on a blanket in front of it.

We each held a glass of chardonnay in our hands.

"I still think it's strange," I said, swirling the liquid in my glass.

"We don't really know anything about them," he said, pointing out the obvious, but staring into the flames, he seemed to be talking mostly to himself.

"I think the house might be haunted," I said, my voice coming out in a whisper.

Cody looked up at me then, holding my gaze. Then he laughed and leaned back on his elbows.

"If it's haunted, they know it," he said.

"But still… I don't think we should let them know that we know."

"Why not?"

"How can you be amused at a time like this?"

"I'm sorry," he said, wiping the grin off his face. All that did was make me smile. "Tell me what evidence you have."

"The phone was unplugged. The painting was stuck."

"Those are normal things," he said.

"I thought I saw a curtain move."

He looked at me through squinted eyes.

"That could be something," he said, with a solemn nod.

"Stop it," I said. "I did see it."

"Okay. Maybe it happened."

I glared at him. "I would rather you didn't agree with me on this."

"Okay," he said. "Tell me about the curtain."

"After I saw it move, I went to the window. I saw you bringing your bicycle around."

"That's it?"

"Yes." I bit my bottom lip to keep from pouting. Then I held up a finger. "Okay. Tell me why the phone only didn't work when Betty was leaving messages.

"I can't really tell you that," he said. "because I don't know."

But I knew that look. He was thinking something.

"What?" I asked, looking at him sideways.

"Just thinking," he said, looking back toward the fire.

That meant he was thinking something he wasn't going to tell me.

After a quick shake of my head, I took a sip of my wine. It was funny, really, how well I knew him—his little mannerisms.

I decided to let it go. I'd figure it out.

And truly, I hoped that I was wrong.

I really hoped that Carlton had gotten Amelia's message and the two of them had tucked it behind the painting together. I did not want to think about alternatives.

Besides, since there was no way to really know, it made sense to choose to think about the most optimistic of the alternatives.

As we sat there, Cody got a text message.

"Everything okay?" I asked as he typed a response.

"Yes," he said. "I have a flight in the morning. Good thing I didn't drink this."

I'd wondered why he'd barely touched his glass of wine.

"Did you know?" I asked. "That you would be flying tomorrow?"

"No." He shook his head. "But I have to always be on call."

Even though it made sense that he would be on call since that was the whole reason he was here—to fly people on and off the island.

But the thought of being on call for six months seemed like a really long time.

CHAPTER 20

Cody

AS I PULLED off my lace-up work boots, I replayed my conversation with Bailey about the house being haunted.

I didn't necessarily believe or disbelieve that a house could be haunted, but I hadn't thought that her evidence was compelling, at least not at first.

But as I put it all together, pieces falling into place, I was beginning to think that she might be onto something.

I wasn't, however, ready to tell her what I was thinking.

First of all, the phone had been unplugged when Betty had tried to call. She had been calling to tell Bailey when I would be here. Since Betty couldn't reach Bailey, it was a surprise for both of us.

Second, the curtains had fluttered luring her to the window when I was beneath it.

Finally the painting had been stuck to the wall until I was back there to catch her. Then it had practically fallen off the wall.

I put on a t-shirt to sleep in and decided that I was being ridiculous.

I was essentially thinking that a ghost or ghosts was playing matchmaker.

If they thought they needed to play matchmaker, they were thinking wrong.

I had already, years ago, been head over heels in love with Bailey. By the time I'd realized it, I had lost touch with her. But now that I had found her, there was no way I was going to let her go again.

I set my alarm and climbed into bed. Fortunately I was used to sleeping in strange places, hotels usually, so I knew I wouldn't have trouble falling asleep.

So much for Betty's prediction that I would be here a week before I had a flight out.

As I drifted off to sleep, it occurred to me that maybe the ghost(s) wasn't playing matchmaker for my benefit, after all, these things had all happened to Bailey, not me, but maybe the ghost was playing matchmaker on her behalf.

Maybe Bailey was the one who needed a little nudging.

That, I decided, would be the thing that a ghost would know about.

I had a lot to think about on my flight tomorrow. Since I didn't have Bailey's cell phone number, I would write her a note.

I'd leave her my cell phone number and ask her to let me know if anything else weird happened with her so-called ghosts.

I didn't want to leave her here alone tomorrow, but that was crazy. She'd been here alone before I got here and she would be fine without me.

The thing was, I wasn't so sure I would be okay without her.

I was smitten… again. Not that I ever got over being smitten by her the first time. I remembered the day we met. Just like it was yesterday.

We'd been in what they had called the computer center, using one of the computers that students used to do homework.

I had been deep into a project and she had been… well… she had been absolutely adorable.

It had been almost eight years ago.

I certainly didn't need anyone, not even a ghost to remind me how much I liked Bailey Lewis.

CHAPTER 21
Bailey — Before

Eight years ago

I HAD A PAPER DUE IN, I glanced at my watch, forty-five minutes.

Stepping into the computer lab on the third floor of the university's business building, I looked around for an unoccupied computer.

The room was hushed, like a library, with only sounds of fingers tapping on computer keyboards, and the whirr and whoosh of a printer.

Nearly two dozen students were crowded into the space of a regular classroom set up with tables around the edge of the room, all facing the wall. A printing station, manned with an older college student, probably a junior or senior, was in the middle of the room.

There was one empty chair on the far side of the room. Hurrying over to snag it, I stashed my backpack next to the computer, pulled out my water bottle, and settled in.

I'd finished writing the paper last night, but I needed to

make one final pass through it and submit it.

I opened the file on my jump drive and began to read, making little edits as I went.

Plenty of time. I had forty minutes.

I was sitting between two guys. The one on my left was quietly reading something on his computer.

The guy on my right had been writing something in a paper notebook, but now he was tapping his pen against the paper.

I attempted to keep my focus on my screen.

I read the same sentence three time.

Tap. Tap. Tap.

"Seriously?" I said with a quick glance in his direction.

The tapping stopped.

But it was too late. My concentration was already shot.

I read the sentence a fourth time.

All I could think about was the guy tapping his pen. Now he was being *too* quiet.

I glanced over at him. He was reading something on his computer screen, but when he saw me looking, he turned his head in my direction and smiled.

I huffed out a breath and glanced at my watch.

Thirty-five minutes now.

I scanned the paper again, knowing I wasn't going to focus enough to get through it again, gave up, and pulled up the course's webpage. Might as well just submit it and be done.

I logged in.

No. I still had time. The classroom was on the second floor, a three minute walk one level down from here. I switched back to the paper and started reading again.

Tap. Tap.

"Is that Business 240?" the guy asked. "I took that one when I was a freshman."

I closed my eyes for a second. Then opened them and looked at him. Really looked at him.

Just like that all my annoyance drained away.

He was smiling at me, but it was his eyes that caught my attention. His blue eyes. Blue as a clear summer sky.

A rush of adrenaline sent my blood rushing through my veins.

"Business 240?" he asked again.

"Yes," I said, turning back to my computer screen.

My hands trembling, now, I uploaded my paper and hit submit.

Thirty minutes. I had thirty minutes to get downstairs to class.

I hit save, logged out, and, ignoring the hot guy sitting next to me, shoved my water bottle into my backpack. Maybe I wasn't exactly ignoring him, but I was putting forth good effort.

I made it as far as the hallway.

"Bailey."

It was him. The annoying guy sitting next to me.

I stopped and turned around. "How do you—"

He held up my jump drive. "You left this."

He held my jump drive, lanyard and badge with my name attached to it.

How had I forgotten that?

I reached out for it, but he pulled it back out of my reach.

"Wait," he said. "What about my reward?"

"What reward?"

He looked at my badge and pretended to read. He had to pretend because there was nothing written there other than my name and phone number.

"The person who finds this drive and returns it will get to walk the owner to her next class."

I crossed my arms.

"What if I wasn't headed to class?"

"I'm sure there is a comparable substitute." He grinned, his kissable lips curving up at the edges.

I bit my lip to keep from smiling.

"Okay," I said, holding out my hand for my jump drive.

He grinned as he placed the lanyard in my hand, then walked in step beside me down the hall toward the stairs.

Suddenly, my three-minute walk to class wasn't nearly long enough.

CHAPTER 22

Cody — Before

IT WAS one of those beautiful fall days when I would rather be in the air than stuck in a computer lab doing homework.

This particular project I was working on wasn't even all that interesting. AGL ceilings. Knots. FAA charts. Very old school. I knew where to find all these calculations. Doing them by hand was just tedious.

When the girl, obviously a college freshman, sat next to me, I was happy for the distraction.

She was so intent, her lips slightly parted, her eyes following the rows of text on the screen. Looking over at her computer, I recognized the topic from my very first business class.

Definitely a first term freshman.

She had her long brunette hair pulled back into a high pony-tail. A university t-shirt, the kind they gave out at orientation.

Going back to my own screen, I found focusing to be a struggle.

"Seriously?" she asked, with a quick glance in my direction.

I held my pen still. I hadn't realized I was tapping my pen.

Now I was definitely not going to get any work done.

All I wanted to do was talk to her.

I watched her for a few minutes more.

Tap. Tap. I couldn't help myself.

"Is that Business 240?" I asked. "I took that one when I was a freshman."

She closed her eyes for a second, then looked at me.

She was cute when she was annoyed. And those eyes were green, a dark green, like Kentucky bluegrass stretching across a field below.

I had flown up to Lexington just last week with my grandfather in one of his Phenoms. He'd let me take the controls. It had been my first time piloting a Phenom and I had been ecstatic.

I was feeling that same rush of adrenalin looking into this girl's eyes.

"Business 240?" I asked again when she didn't answer.

"Yes," she said, looking back her screen.

This girl was stunningly beautiful. I logged off the computer and stared at my paper, trying to think of a way to talk to her that wouldn't annoy her so much.

Maybe if I just waited until she was finished. I could be a patient man when I needed to be.

Then in a sudden flash of movement, she logged off the computer and grabbing up her backpack, rushed across the room toward the door.

But she had left something behind.

I tugged her jump drive out of the computer and while I followed her across the room, I noticed her name on the badge.

Fate. It had to be fate.

"Bailey," I called out just as she entered the hallway.

"How do you—" She stopped and turned around, that annoyed—vexed—expression on her face.

I held up her jump drive. "You left this."

When she reached for it, I pulled it back. There was no way I was letting this opportunity pass.

"Wait," I said. "What about my reward?"

"What reward?"

I looked at her badge. "The person who finds this drive and returns it will get to walk the owner to her next class."

I crossed my arms. "It does not say that."

"No? I think it's right here."

"What if I wasn't headed to class?" she said. I could see from her expression that I had won.

"I'm sure there is a comparable substitute." I could walk her home. To the student union. Anywhere.

"Okay," she said, holding out her hand.

I dropped the lanyard into her hand, then stepped in beside her as she walked down the hallway.

"I'm Cody," I said.

"Hi Cody," she said, smiling at me.

I nearly missed a step. She wasn't looking vexed anymore, but her smile was more beautiful than a ray of sunshine shooting through a patch of cumulus clouds on a clear spring morning.

And that was saying something.

CHAPTER 23
Bailey

WHEN I GOT up the next morning, Cody was gone.

I knew because he had left me a note, written on the top sheet of one of my legal pads, on the table.

Dear Bailey,

I realized that we don't have each other's cell phone numbers.

Here is mine: 409-753-7593.

Call if you need anything or have any trouble with ghosts. If I can't get there, I can send someone.

I should be home mid-afternoon.

Cody

The sun was barely up, still splashing the sky in red as I jogged along the path toward town.

My running shoes pounded the pavement, the 80s music I usually listened to when I went running was silent, my air pods in my pocket.

I listened instead to the sound of water lapping against the shore, the birds singing their morning song, and the mournful wail of the ferry's horn drifting across the water. The ferry would be bringing tourists, the first ones for the day.

As I hit the pavement of Main Street, I noticed it was still quiet. Most people who stayed overnight weren't up yet and the first ferry was on its way.

I liked the crowds and the delight and wonder the tourists brought, but I also like the quiet.

Going into the coffee shop, I ordered a small cappuccino and took it outside to stand on the boardwalk to look out over the water.

When I heard the distinct sound of a private plane overhead, a swarm of butterflies let loose in my stomach.

Leaning against the wooden railing, I watched the airplane —a Skye Travels Phenom—make a low sweep over the Grand Hotel before it gained altitude as it passed Main Street, then headed off toward the horizon.

It was Cody. I knew it just as sure as I knew my own name.

He would not have seen me. I was wearing a baseball cap and a running outfit he wouldn't recognize.

I watched until the airplane was nothing but a speck in the sky. I watched until my eyes burned from trying to follow the airplane with me eyes until it was out of sight.

I should be home mid-afternoon. That's what his note had said.

Home.

I tossed my almost empty coffee cup into a trash can as I shifted into a jog heading back toward the house. There was a road that went all the way around the island, but I wasn't ready to tackle that just yet. Not by myself anyway.

Maybe with Cody.

He'd said he'd be *home*.

Those six years since he'd left College Station may as well have not even passed.

I had simply been existing. Waiting for Cody.

And I hadn't even known it.

I stuck my air pods in my ears and lost myself in some good 80s music.

After all this time, I was still in love with Cody Johnson.

CHAPTER 24

Cody

TODAY'S FLIGHT WAS EASY.

I was going to pick up a teenager in Chicago to bring out to the island for the summer. A common thing, I was sure.

The island wouldn't be a bad place for a teenager to spend a summer.

I didn't know how many teens actually lived on the island, but surely there were some.

I made a pass over the Grand Hotel and Main Street before gaining altitude.

There weren't too many people out on the island this morning. But before long the ferries would start bringing in the tourists.

I liked thinking about Bailey there waiting for me.

At home.

I'd smiled as I'd written the note to Bailey. Wondered if she would notice.

I hoped she'd send me a text soon just so I would have her cell phone number. The only way I could get in touch with her right now was to call Betty who had her landline number.

And then there was no guarantee that the phone would ring.

Couldn't very well ring when the ghosts kept unplugging the phone from the wall.

Maybe it was Amelia, I mused. Maybe she was there, trying to help Bailey find her soulmate.

I didn't mind a little help wherever I could get it, even if it was from a ghost.

Thinking about Bailey, replaying our day together yesterday, kept my mind occupied for the flight over to Chicago.

It was like no time at all had passed and yet at the same time it was like everything was new with her.

I'd thought about her kisses over the years, but like all memories, they had faded. I was left wondering what her kisses would taste like now.

Would our kisses hold the same passion they'd held all those years ago when we were young or would they be different? Had the years put a distance between us that we wouldn't be able to overcome?

I couldn't imagine that it would if yesterday was any indication.

Just holding her hand had nearly been more than I could bear.

I'd wanted to pull her into a kiss, especially last night when we had sat in front of the fireplace.

But I didn't want to rush things. I wanted to do things right.

But what was right?

How did a man go about courting the woman he already knew he wanted to be with?

Was it flowers and dinners? Did one of those dinners need to involve a flight somewhere?

Was it simply moonlight walks along the shore of Lake Huron?

I needed to talk to my Grandpa. He would know.

In the meantime, it seemed like the best thing to do was to keep things simple.

Sitting in front of the fireplace with a glass of wine after a walk in the moonlight.

I had to let her know that I was in it for the long run. That I wasn't just a fly by night kind of guy.

Unfortunately, my history with her might suggest the opposite.

It didn't even factor in for me that she had been the one to stop answering the telephone. She had merely been protecting herself. I didn't hold that against her at all.

My instinct told me to move slowly with her. To give her time to trust me again.

And my grandfather had taught me to always follow my instinct whether it was in the cockpit or with a woman.

CHAPTER 25

Bailey

AFTER MY MORNING JOG, I spent the rest of the day in my second-floor office, working on a marketing plan for a company in Houston.

Part of that time had been spent on the phone with the client. He was a guy from France opening a French restaurant in River Oaks.

I didn't particularly like him as a person—he was narcissistic and came in with preconceived notions of how things should be done, things that were not in his best interest.

But I was a professional and I didn't have to like him. I just had to understand his vision for his company. And that part I understood. He was targeting an upscale clientele. Young. Professional.

I was lost in my project when I heard the door open downstairs.

I tapped my phone to check the time. Four fifteen.

Mid-afternoon. Sort of.

I hoped, since I had given him the code to the door, that it was Cody.

Since I was deep into finishing up a section, I put my head back down and kept going.

Or at least that was my plan.

After five minutes, I had to give up.

It reminded me of that first day when I'd met Cody. He had distracted me away from doing my work then, too. He was a very distracting person.

I straightened up my workspace and headed downstairs.

I followed the distinctive sound of someone chopping vegetables into the kitchen.

I held my breath as I reached the door. If it was a ghost, I was going to leave.

But it wasn't a ghost. It was Cody.

He was chopping up green peppers and tossing them into a pan.

"Hi," I said.

"Hi." He stopped, looked up, and smiled. "I hope I didn't disturb you."

"Not at all," I lied. He hadn't done anything to disturb me other than to just be here. "You're cooking."

"Hope you like stir fry," he said.

"Of course I do." He should know that. How many times had we eaten Chinese together? But then homemade stir fry—homemade anything—hadn't been something either of us had access to do at the time. We lived in student housing and mostly ate in the student union.

Actually, I was the one who usually ate in the student union. Anytime we ate together, we got in his car and went somewhere off-campus. It was funny. This was the first time I'd really realized this.

"Sit," he said. "I'll get you a glass of wine."

"What can I do to help?" I asked, sliding onto one of the bar stools on the other side of the island.

"You can keep me company," he said, pouring wine into a glass and sliding it over to me.

"Where did all this food come from?" I asked.

He shrugged. "I had a little time in Chicago, so I did some grocery shopping. You seemed to be missing a few things."

That was an understatement since I hadn't cooked in this kitchen even once. I couldn't decide if I wanted to admit that to him or not.

"How was your flight?"

"Uneventful," he said.

"The best kind."

He grinned. "Any ghostly activity?"

I shook my head. "Not yet."

"There's still time," he said, over his shoulder as he filled a pot with water.

"It would be okay with me if we don't have any."

He just smiled. I could tell there was something he wasn't telling me. I just didn't know what it was. Not yet.

CHAPTER 26

Cody

"DO YOU HAVE A FLIGHT TOMORROW?" Bailey asked. "scheduled?"

"Not yet. Especially not if it keeps raining."

We sat in front of the fireplace, but on the sofa tonight.

I liked how this was already becoming a routine. Our routine.

After dinner, we'd cleaned up the kitchen, then came into the living room.

It was raining. Not hard, but enough of a steady mist to keep us from taking a walk.

"I don't remember you ever mentioning your aunt," I said.

"I probably didn't," I said. "I was at that age where I didn't want anyone to know I had family."

I laughed. "I remember those days." Mine had been selective though. Parents definitely. And siblings. But I'd never really felt that way about my grandparents.

It was funny though, that even though I hadn't felt that way about my grandparents, I hadn't talked about them. I hadn't wanted anyone to think that I wasn't making my own way. I didn't want anyone to think that was riding on my family's coattails. Everything I did, I did on my own. Since my last name was Johnson and not Worthington, it made it easy to keep people from knowing that my grandfather was the founder and owner of Skye Travels—one of Houston's multi-billionaires.

Grandpa Noah would not have allowed us to coast on his name anyway.

He only hired us on at Skye Travels if we were as good as or even better than anyone else outside of the family that he hired.

Everyone who cared to notice knew that he was actually harder on us than on nonfamily members.

He didn't hide the fact that he hired family, but he made sure that everyone he hired was qualified—more than qualified.

I hadn't even told Bailey about my family connection. The problem with that was now I had to figure out a way to tell her that wouldn't make her feel like I'd been being deceptive.

It made sense that I wouldn't tell her in college.

And now she was making assumptions that I worked for Skye Travels. I did work for Skye Travels. And every Sunday our family got together at my grandparents. Rarely all at once, but whoever happened to be available.

Maybe that was the answer.

"You seem deep in thought," she said.

"I was just thinking," I said.

She raised an eyebrow. "What are you thinking about?"

"Are you busy Sunday?"

"Sunday? I don't know. I guess not."

"Want to take a flight to Houston? My grandparents are having an outdoor barbecue and the weather is supposed to be nice."

"Sure," she said. "That sounds nice."

One step forward.

One step at the time.

I had three days to figure out where to go from here.

CHAPTER 27

Bailey

THE RAIN WAS COMING DOWN STEADY NOW, pounding against the windows. I liked a good storm as long as I could be inside to watch from the cozy dry warmth of indoors.

Cody and I sat on either end of the sofa—the big one in the living room, our feet on the ottoman, the fire quietly burning in the fireplace.

We were a little like an old married couple, I mused, except that we'd probably be watching television or reading. We were still enjoying just sitting and talking.

It was nice actually. I didn't feel pressured to keep a conversation going. We just chatted here and there on things as they occurred to us.

Then just when things were getting comfortable, Cody went and threw a kink in things. That was just how he was.

In the two years that we had dated, I had never met his parents. He'd gone home a lot. I did know that. But he had never asked me to go with him.

I couldn't tell him no. I didn't want to tell him no.

I was still trying to figure out where we were headed in this second go around of a relationship. Avoiding his family at this point would not be a good idea.

And I was curious. But at the same time, maybe even more so, I was nervous.

What would his family be like?

I suspected they would be somewhat wealthy. Maybe upper middle class. It was a well-known fact that aviation majors almost always came from wealthy families. Either that or they worked part-time to pay for all the extra fees required for flying.

Cody had not worked in college. I was certain of that. He'd either been in class, in an airplane, or with me. That didn't leave any time for working.

It was possible, though, that he had a lot of student loan debt.

But either way, I had to err on the side of caution and assume that his family was well off.

That didn't bother me except that now I had to figure out what to wear.

What exactly did a girl wear to a family barbecue? I hadn't even brought all my clothes. They were in my apartment in Dallas.

Even if it was logical to ask him to stop in Dallas for me to get some of my clothes—which it was not, I still wouldn't know what to wear.

I could ask him. But would he know?

If he was like most guys, he'd just say it didn't matter.

"Now you're deep in thought," he said.

I sighed. If we were going to do this thing, we had to be open.

I was convinced that if both of us had been more open when we were in college, we would have ended up together back then instead of drifting apart.

"I need to go into town. See if they have something appropriate for a barbecue with the family." There. That was about as sideways a question as I could come up with.

"You don't have your clothes here?"

"Only a few."

"A shopping trip in Mackinac sounds like fun."

Cody and I had never been shopping together.

We were getting into the new part of our relationship.

"Tomorrow then," I said. "if you don't have a flight."

"I won't have a flight," he said.

When I looked over at him sideways, he just grinned innocently at me.

I made a face. There was nothing innocent about Cody Johnson.

CHAPTER 28
Cody

THE NEXT MORNING was bright and sunny. Not hot and sunny like Texas, but pleasantly sunny. The rain had moved out, leaving everything smelling fresh.

Fresh grass, magnolia blooms, even the sand along the shore seemed cleaner.

Or maybe it wasn't so much fresh and clean as it was the way I was seeing things.

Being here with Bailey made me just flat out happy.

It was mid-morning as we walked along the sidewalk toward town. The water lapping gently against the shore.

The deep, mournful drawn out blast of the ferry's horn announced that it would be leaving soon. I only knew this because a line formed at the gate to get on the boat.

"Have you ever ridden the ferry?" I asked.

"Of course," she said. "It's how I got here."

"Right." Since taking a ferry or taking an airplane were the only two ways to get here, it was a stupid question.

"Have you?"

"No," I said. And, truly, why would I? That would be like driving from here to Texas and that wasn't going to happen.

"We should take the ferry over to the mainland," she said. "It's nice."

"Okay." Maybe driving would happen. Apparently ferry rides were going to happen.

She smiled. I was enamored and I knew it.

We stepped into the first clothing store we came to. It was actually the only clothing store that sold anything other than t-shirts. I had googled it.

There were a couple of people wandering about, but it was quiet inside. No music. The old wooden floor creaked under the weight of our footsteps.

"Let me know if you need help with anything," the clerk behind the counter said, barely looking up from her phone. She looked like a college student, unconcerned, really, about the customers.

Bailey wandered aimlessly for few minutes, not saying anything, then she stopped and turned to face me.

"You have sisters, right?" she asked.

"Yes. And cousins. And aunts."

She nodded, looking a little pale for a second.

"What do they wear to these family barbecues?"

I grinned. It hadn't occurred to me until now that she would be worried about what to wear. But of course she would.

"Would you like me to pick something out?" I asked.

"Sure," she said, but she was looking at me with obvious skepticism.

I rubbed my hands together and grinned.

"This is going to be fun," I said. "Trust me."

"Oh no." She put a hand over her eyes, then smiled.

It didn't take me long to find two possible outfits that would allow her to fit right in with the other females in my family.

"Do you have a dressing room?" I asked the clerk.

"Sure," the college student said, hopping off her stool and leading us to the back of the store where she unlocked the door to the dressing room.

I handed Bailey the clothes I'd picked out.

"I'll wait out here," I said as she stepped inside the dressing room and closed the door.

I paced into the store, then back.

"Are you going to let me see?" I asked her through the closed door.

"Maybe," she said, her voice muffled.

I grinned.

I hadn't even known how much I'd missed her.

CHAPTER 29

Bailey

IT WAS a little disconcerting to know that Cody was waiting outside the door while I tried on clothes he had picked out.

The first one was a flowy skirt splashed with blue flowers that almost reached my ankles in the back. It was several inches shorter in the front. The top he'd picked out was also in a blue that blended in with the different blues in the skirt. I was rather impressed with his eye for color. The white lightweight cardigan pulled it all together.

"Are you going to let me see?" he asked, through the door, as I pulled the top over my head.

"Maybe," I said, then once I was dressed, I studied my reflection and decided that I could show him.

Taking a deep breath, I opened the door and stepped out in my bare feet.

"Wow," he said.

"You like it?"

"Come look in the big mirror," he said.

I stood in front of the three-way mirror and turned so that the skirt flowed around me.

"You have to get this one," he said.

"Okay," I said, smiling over at him. I had to agree. "I should put on the other one."

Back in the dressing room, feeling better about the whole thing, I changed into the other skirt and top.

I was feeling better now that I knew what I was expected to wear. And I felt comfortable in the outfit. It wasn't something like I usually wore, especially since I mostly worked from home, but I liked it and it felt right.

The other outfit was an emerald green satin skirt, also in high low style, but it had a front side slit up to there. It, too, had bold flowers but these were in pinks and oranges here and there. Another white shirt, this one a v-neck, and a blue-jean jacket to go over it. I decided I liked this outfit, too.

I stepped out of the dressing room door where Cody was leaning against the doorframe looking the other way.

"Cody," I said.

He turned around and looked at me. Then he shook his head.

"Nope," he said, putting a hand over his chin. "Not this one."

I walked to the mirror and turned this way and that. I honestly didn't see what he didn't like about it.

"What's wrong with it?" I asked, looking over at him, perplexed.

"Absolutely nothing," he said. "But not for the barbeque. This is something to wear to dinner."

"Dinner?"

"We'll go to the Grand Hotel for dinner tomorrow night. This is perfect."

"The Grand Hotel?"

"Formal attire is required."

He had me speechless. I forced myself to close my mouth.

"I have a blue jean jacket," I said, although I honestly didn't know why I felt the need to tell him.

"Here or in Dallas?"

"Dallas," I said.

"Well, now you'll have two."

I went back into the dressing room and changed back into my jeans and sweatshirt.

Belatedly, I checked the prices. Tourist prices, I thought, grateful I had the money Betty had sent me for Cody's rent.

"What size shoe do your wear?" he asked, as I left the dressing room.

"Six, but…" I couldn't help but think about how much shoes much cost here.

"Here," he said, "let me hold these. You try on these shoes." He held up a pair of white canvas sneakers.

"I have shoes like that," I said, relieved that I wasn't expected to buy anything else.

"Okay," he said, putting the shoes down.

I followed him to the checkout counter and watched as the girl rang up the purchases.

To distract myself, I looked at the display of necklaces on the counter, stopping to examine a little locket in the shape of a heart.

As the girl bagged up the clothes, I unzipped my purse to pull out my credit card.

"Here you go," she said, handing the bag with handles over to Cody.

"But I—"

"It's taken care of," Cody told me, then thanked the clerk.

I had no choice but to follow him outside.

Obviously Cody had just bought me two very pricey outfits.

CHAPTER 30

Cody

THE TOWN WAS CROWDED NOW. As summer approached, it seemed to get more crowded every day.

Since there were two more ferries on the schedule than there were just a couple of days ago, I was pretty sure it wasn't just an illusion.

Bailey and I stepped out of the dress shop into the bright sunlight.

When I reached automatically for her hand, she pulled back, tugging my hand. I turned and looked into her eyes.

It took all my self-control not to smile. She was wearing that vexed expression that made her exceptionally adorable. The one she had given me that first day we'd met when I had been tapping my pen.

That had been almost eight years ago and I hadn't been able to tap a pen on a piece of paper without thinking of her since that day.

"What is it, Chère?" I asked.

She crossed her arms. I had no choice but to grin.

"You bought me clothes." It sounded like an accusation.

"Yes," I said, like a confession. "Yes, I did."

"You're not supposed to do that."

"Who says?"

"It's not proper," she said after a moment's hesitation.

"Proper?" I laughed. "Come on, Southern girl." I took her hand. "Let me buy you lunch."

It was almost impossible to talk as we walked along the crowded street.

We ducked into a decent looking restaurant and the hostess led us to a little table by the window.

"Why?" she asked.

I knew what she was asking. She was still on the clothes I'd bought her.

"Because I'm the one who invited you. It seemed like the least I could do."

She picked up her menu. "That's warped," she said.

"How is it warped?" I asked, amused.

The server came and brought us water. "Anything else?" he asked.

Bailey shook her head.

"We're good," I said, picking up my menu, glancing at it, and setting it aside.

"How long do you plan on being vexed with me?"

"I'm not vexed." She lowered her menu and looked at me.

She was vexed. I could see it in her eyes. When she was vexed, her eyes took on an even deeper shade of green.

"Okay," I said. "Good. What would you like to eat?"

She set her menu aside and leaned forward. "Why?" she asked. "Why would you buy me things?"

I suppose it was a valid question, although I didn't really understand it. I hadn't thought she was one of those women who got offended when a man held the door for her or bought her something nice.

"Because I can," I said. It was about as honest an answer as I could give her.

"We aren't even dating," she said, sitting back in her chair and holding her menu in front of her.

I reached over and nudged it down.

"We could be," I said. "We should be."

At least she didn't look vexed anymore. Now she just looked downright confused.

"What?"

"Who decides?" I asked.

"Who... decides... what?"

"Who decided if we're dating?"

"I guess we do." A little smile was playing about the corner of her lips and I knew I'd distracted her away from worrying about me buying her a few clothes.

"Okay." I said, holding out a hand. "Then we're dating. Let's shake on it."

She laughed, but she did not shake my hand. "You can't shake on something like that."

"Why not?"

"Because it's not..." She narrowed her eyes at me. "It doesn't fit the context."

"What does?" I asked. "Tell me what to do."

She picked up her glass of water and took a sip.

"Let's just order something," she said.

CHAPTER 31

Bailey

ONE OF US WAS INSANE. Either me or Cody. Maybe both.

We were sitting in a crowded restaurant, music playing overhead, lots of conversations swirling around.

A server passed by with a tray held high of what looked like seafood. Smelled like seafood, too. I was pretty sure I saw French fries, along with whatever else it was.

Cody had just declared us to be dating. And then he wanted to shake on it.

"You can't shake on a decision to date," I said, looking at him as though he were daft. "That's what you do when you make a business deal."

I looked toward the ceiling and blew out a breath. Cody knew these things. He wasn't stupid. He was just toying with me.

"It's not a business deal?" he asked.

"I certainly hope not."

"Then…?"

"It's a relationship."

"How are we supposed to seal the deal?"

First of all, I had not agreed to date him. Second of all, I hadn't not agreed to date him. I had already been trying to figure out where this relationship was going. He wasn't supposed to just decide. Was he?

"You're thinking too much," he said.

The server came and took our orders.

"It bears thinking about," I said.

He tried to look serious. I had to give him that.

I had lost track of who was toying with who.

It occurred to me then that we were toying with each other.

I put my elbows on the table and leaned forward.

"Are you saying you want to date me?" I asked.

"We're going to the Grand Hotel tomorrow," he said. "That's a date."

"No," I said, shaking my head. "You *told* me. You didn't ask me. You have to ask for it to be a date."

"Okay," he said. "You don't want to have dinner at the Grand Hotel?"

"That's not the point."

He grinned at me. "Will you have dinner with me at the Grand Hotel tomorrow?"

I closed my eyes a moment. I had a feeling that my life was spinning out of control and I couldn't do anything to stop it. Thing was, I wasn't sure I wanted to.

I was probably going to regret it, but...

"Yes," I said.

"Good. Sounds like we're dating."

I just looked at him. Maybe flying around in all that thin air had done something to his brain.

"I'll leave it up to you to figure out what we need to do to seal the deal."

I laughed and started organizing the little pink and blue sweetener and sugar packets in the white holder.

"You're laughing."

"No choice," I said. "You're messed up."

"Can't deny that," he said. "When you figure out the answer, let me know."

Finished with my organization task, I slid the white sugar packet holder aside.

"I already know the answer," I said quickly with a glance at the tourists walking outside the window, some of them looking in at us.

He grinned. "Please share, Chère," he said.

It was hard to think straight when he was using French words of endearment on me. He knew it was one of my weaknesses. He had to know.

He had to remember.

CHAPTER 32

Cody

I KNEW PERFECTLY WELL that a handshake was not the proper way to agree to date someone.

I also knew that it was usually either a tacit agreement or a simple question. With adults, it seemed to be more often a tacit agreement than anything else.

Either a tacit agreement or an engagement ring.

Since I didn't have an engagement ring on hand and I didn't feel like a tacit agreement was enough for us at this point, I wanted her to tell what would be appropriate.

Just as she did, I also knew the answer.

But I wanted her to tell me.

It had to be her idea. I wanted—needed—it to be her idea. And it wasn't for me. It was for her. I wanted her to feel like she was the one in charge of the relationship.

I never, however, agreed to let her off the easy way.

I leaned forward and whispered. "You don't have to tell me now, Chère. You can tell me later."

She was looking vexed again.

She narrowed her eyes at me, then sat back and looked away.

I sat back, too, and sipped my water.

When she met my gaze again, she was smiling.

"You're just trying to mess with my head," she said.

"Why would I do that?"

"I don't really know," she said, her brow creased. "Because you can."

I laughed. "Good point," I said.

I didn't bother to tell her the only reason I could possibly mess with her head was because she let me.

"You're incorrigible," she said.

"I know. That's one of the things you love about me."

She sat very still, not moving a muscle.

Since my phone had been vibrating in my pocket for a few minutes now, I decided that now was the time to check it.

It was a text from Charlotte.

CHARLOTTE

Will you be coming to Houston this weekend?

How was it that women had such bad timing? Was it instinct or something?

I don't know. Why?

I saw your mother at Nordstrom's. She asked if I'd be at the barbecue this Sunday. Mentioned you'll be there.

And why, I wanted to point out, would you be asking when you already knew the answer?

I flicked a glance up at Bailey. She was sipping her water and trying not pay attention to what I was doing.

Don't do that.

Thought bubbles.

The server brought our food and I put my phone away.

Good God. This was a disaster waiting to happen. And my own mother had set it in motion.

"Everything okay?" Bailey asked.

"Yeah," I said. "It's nothing."

I would worry about Charlotte later.

I would not let her ruin a perfectly good day with Bailey.

Unfortunately, even with Bailey looking at me with one delicate eyebrow raised, it was hard not to think about what I was going to do to fix this thing.

She knew something was up. Charlotte knew something was up. Since I hadn't gotten around to sending her that message that we weren't going to be seeing each other anymore, I couldn't put the blame on her.

I couldn't even blame my mother, although that would have been easy to do.

What a mess I was suddenly tangled up in.

CHAPTER 33

Bailey

CODY HAD me so off balance, it was all I could do to eat at all. And this place had really good French fries. Instead of ketchup, they had some kind of fry sauce. Not half bad.

First of all, he'd been bantering around the words Chère and love like they were nothing. Then he'd gotten a text that he had not been expecting.

Girlfriend maybe.

Whoever it was, not only did he not want to talk about it, it took the playfulness out of his mood and he went quiet.

It was unfortunate.

After we finished eating lunch, I looked at my watch.

"I have some work I need to get done today," I said. It wasn't entirely false. I always had work I could do. I had also had a lot of flexibility and the work could wait.

"Okay," Cody said, not even trying to talk me into staying into town a little longer.

That told me that whoever had sent that text was important.

I also knew, even though he had put his phone back in his pocket, that he was still getting text messages. I could hear it vibrating.

We walked home in silence.

The water lapping against the shore was the same. The ferry's mournful horn echoing across the water was the same. The chipmunks skittering across the sidewalk in front of us was the same. Even the white birds swooping into the water, the others calling out what sounded like encouraging squawks.

But something was different.

Cody was preoccupied, checking his messages occasionally, but not answering.

Our conversation about dating seemed to have been forgotten.

I told myself it didn't matter. I told myself that he and I weren't really dating.

That we were just here together by happenstance.

It didn't mean that we were just going to wipe away the last six years of our lives and pick up where we left off even if it did seem like it at times.

We turned right to head down the sidewalk toward the house.

Trying to act like everything was normal, even though it clearly wasn't, I looked up at the windows of the house.

The curtains in my bedroom fluttered. I slowed down. I had not left my window open. I never left my window open. Being from Texas, it just wasn't something I did. With the heat and humidity, it was rarely an option.

Then I stopped and put a hand on Cody's arm.

I wanted to say something, but I couldn't form the words.

He turned back and looked at me.

"What's—"

He turned and followed the direction of my gaze.

The curtains fluttered again.

And she was gone.

"Did you see her?" I asked, my voice barely more than a whisper.

"Yes," he said. "But only for a moment."

I had seen a ghost. Amelia maybe. My gut told me it was

Amelia. Surely the house wasn't full of ghosts. One would be more than enough.

Whoever she was, she had barely been more than a shape. An ethereal presence. Not an actual person. But I'd seen her clearly enough to tell that she had long hair that fell over her shoulders and she had been looking straight out over the water, staring straight ahead.

She should have been too far away to tell, but I somehow knew that she looked sad. Heartbroken even.

Cody took my hand. "Come on," he said. "Let's go inside."

I shook my head. "I don't know."

"Why not? Are you scared of ghosts?" I could tell he was trying to make light of it, but I also heard the trepidation in his voice.

"Maybe. That's my bedroom."

CHAPTER 34

Cody

IN SPITE of my attempt to not let Charlotte ruin my day with Bailey, it had anyway.

Not only had I gotten texts from Charlotte asking about the barbecue on Sunday, but also my mother sent me a message telling me that Charlotte was going to be there.

That was the message that left me immobilized.

Now I had to not only figure out how to tell Charlotte not to come, I had to tell my mother that Charlotte could *not* come to the barbecue.

Even though I might try to play it off otherwise, I was a gentleman.

And I didn't like hurting anyone. Not even Charlotte. I liked her. I just didn't want to be with her anymore. And I certainly didn't want to marry her.

But now I had a quandary. I'd already invited Bailey and she had agreed to go with me.

No matter what I did about Charlotte, there was a risk that Charlotte would show up anyway. That would be a disaster as far as Bailey went.

"Cody."

Bailey reached out and put a hand on my arm, stopping me.

I hadn't said a word on the walk home and I hadn't even realized it until this moment.

When I turned and saw the expression on Bailey's face, my blood had run cold.

Expecting to see that someone had broken into the house or maybe even flames shooting from the roof, I turned and looked in the same direction she was looking.

I saw just the flash of an image of a girl, then the flutter of curtains.

Amelia. It had to be.

And she didn't want me to see her.

But she wanted Bailey to see her.

Why?

I tried to lighten the situation, but that wasn't happening.

"That's my bedroom," Bailey said.

Nope. I did not blame her. If that was my bedroom, I wouldn't be staying in it either.

"Okay," I said. "Well. We can't stay out here."

I tugged her arm and she took a step forward.

"Bailey," I said, with more force.

She blinked and looked at me.

"I don't think she'll hurt you."

"I don't care."

I didn't care either. I could not in good conscience let Bailey stay up there in that bedroom by herself when there might be a ghost living up there.

"We'll move you downstairs," I said.

She nodded slowly. "Okay."

Together we went inside the house.

Everything felt perfectly normal to me.

The landline was still plugged in. I took that as a good sign.

Bailey stood in the middle of the living room and stared at the painting on the wall. The one of the newlyweds from the 1800s.

"I'll just put your clothes in my room," I said. "You can sleep in there."

"Okay," she said, but didn't take her eyes off the painting.

I didn't know what she was expecting to see. Maybe she was trying to see if the image of Amelia was the same as the ghost she had seen.

I didn't know. I had to move Bailey's things downstairs, but first I had a couple of phone calls to make.

CHAPTER 35

Bailey

I **SET** up my MacBook on the kitchen table and answered a few emails in an attempt to ease myself into doing some work. There were several hours left in the work day and, having a strong work ethic, I was strict on myself.

Unless I had a good reason, like taking a few hours to go into town to do some shopping with Cody, I showed up for work. Even with taking long lunches, I still managed to get in a good eight hours of work most days.

Finding out there was a ghost in the house—in my bedroom—and having to relocate both my office and bedroom to the first floor put a kink in my work day.

Cody had bravely gone upstairs to retrieve my computer before stepping outside. Even now, I watched him pacing back and forth on the back deck. He was wearing cordless air pods, but he was obviously deep in conversation.

With my gaze repeatedly wandering in his direction, I gave up and watched him.

When I'd known him before, he had been a handsome upperclassman, lean and walked with purpose and a bit of swagger wherever he went.

Now he was still handsome, even more so—I had not

thought that would have been possible six years ago—still lean although filled out in places I wouldn't have known needed filling out.

There was one interesting thing I noticed as he paced back and forth—something that I was just now consciously registering.

Some of the swagger in his gait had smoothed out. He walked with more confidence now. More confidence. Less swagger.

And yet the mere sight of him still made my heart flutter.

Even though he and I had been attached at the hip for my first two years of college, I'd always been a little bit wary of him. There were things he hadn't shared with me. Including his family.

I didn't fault him for it. I hadn't talked much about my family either.

But now, right out of the chute, he was taking me to meet his family. Not just his parents, but his grandparents and possibly a whole bunch of his extended family.

Chewing on the end of my pen, I wondered why.

What was different? Two days had passed now and he obviously had some things in his life that needed to be worked out.

He stopped pacing, put his hands on his hips, and stared in my direction, his head slightly tipped to the side.

There was something different about him, but I needed to keep my wits about me. I couldn't just go falling head over heels for him. Again.

I didn't know what the future held for either of us. He was scheduled to be here for six months. I was supposed to have already packed up the house and headed back to Texas.

I'd gotten comfortable. I blamed part of it on Cody or rather Betty from Houston. I couldn't very well put the house on the market during the six months they were renting it.

And yet even as easy as it was to blame them for my still being here, I couldn't. It wasn't fair to them.

It was my own doing.

I liked it here.

But would I like it here after Cody left in six months?

The clock chimed the hour. Five o'clock.

I closed my computer. I wasn't getting work done. I might as well do something constructive. Something that didn't require a lot of brain power.

Cody was pacing again.

I couldn't remember him ever doing that when we were college students. But then I wouldn't have known if he did.

We were practically living together now and we were learning things about each other that we might not ever have known otherwise.

Living together.

The thought of living with Cody had me feeling a bit weak in the knees.

I needed to put Cody out of my head and think about something else.

I blew out a breath as I went to get a glass of water.

Like that was going to happen.

CHAPTER 36

Cody

I FOUND Bailey in the walk-in pantry, tossing cans into a box.

I'd spent the last hour or so talking first to my mother, then Charlotte. The first conversation had just been weird. The second conversation was just plain uncomfortable.

At least I could tell my mother straight out that I didn't want to see Charlotte anymore. She had apologized, but I had the sense that Charlotte had rather pushed herself into the invitation.

When Charlotte and I had first started dating, I had taken her to a charity function where she had met my parents. It had been during the holidays and I hadn't wanted to go by myself.

Charlotte had obviously given meeting my parents more weight than I had. Again. Not her fault. I hadn't told her anything one way or the other.

At any rate, my mother now knew that I was bringing Bailey home Sunday. She remembered Bailey. I'd talked about her in college, even though I had never brought her home.

Charlotte, I suspected, I would never talk to again.

Bailey, sitting on a step stool, looked up at me.

"What's this?" I asked.

"Donations," she said. "I don't really cook, so..." She shrugged.

I knelt down and picked up a can of corn.

"I do cook, but I prefer to cook with fresh ingredients."

She added a can of beans to the box.

"We could use this tomato sauce," I said, picking up a red can.

"I kept some of those," she said, nodding toward a section on one of the shelves with a few other cans of tomato sauce and a bottle of ketchup. "just in case."

I added the can I had rescued from the box to the shelf.

"Hey," she said, clasping her hands together in her lap and looking into my eyes.

I waited.

"I don't have to go Sunday. If something else came up, I understand."

Observation had always been one of Bailey's strong abilities.

"It was a misunderstanding, that's all," I said.

She nodded. "But really. We can do it another time."

I glanced around the pantry. It had one light in the ceiling and we were surrounded by more cans and bottles than an army could eat in a month. It wasn't exactly the most romantic place.

"Bailey," I said. "Will you come outside with me for a minute?"

"Okay,"

I pulled her up off the step stool and we went outside into the cool evening air.

I had something I needed to do and even though the timing was right, the place wasn't. A pantry full of canned goods was not the right place.

CHAPTER 37

Bailey

I WALKED along the shoreline with Cody. The sun hadn't dropped over the horizon yet, but it was poised, sending out its array of bright colors in anticipation.

The neighbor and his husky walked several yards ahead of us.

But it was quiet. Just the steady lapping of the water against the sand.

"Is this about the ghost?" I asked, thinking that was a good reason for Cody to want to get out of the house.

He smiled. "No, but we do need to bring your things downstairs."

I shivered. "Would have been good to do that before it got dark."

"We have electric lights," he said, playfully bumping his shoulder against mine.

"I know," I said. "But still…"

"Don't worry. Just tell me what you need and I'll go up to get it."

"Okay," I said.

"Hey. You agreed far too quickly to just send me up there alone."

"I don't want to keep you from being my knight in shining armor," I said.

"Alright," he said. "I'll do it. But just for you."

"I would hope you wouldn't do it for just anybody."

"Don't worry," he said. "You're it."

We walked in silence a few minutes. It seemed like an odd thing for him to say and I wasn't sure how to respond.

Something still seemed to be bothering him.

I looked down. Watched the way our feet, both of us wearing lace-up boots, moved in tandem.

"I'm sorry I stopped answering your calls."

He took my hand. "You don't have to apologize. We were young and didn't know what we wanted. At least I didn't."

"We were young," I agreed, looking away.

"It didn't take me long to figure it out though," he said. "I looked for you."

I glanced up at him. I hadn't dared to think that he might look for me.

"I got a new cell phone number when I got back to Dallas."

"I see."

I took a deep breath and squeezed his hand. "I looked for you, too."

"I guess neither one of us is very active on social media."

"I guess not," I said.

"Bailey," he said. "Have you ever known me not to keep my word?"

I thought for a few minutes. "No," I said, softly.

"I asked you to go to the barbeque. You're the one I want there with me."

I nodded. My heart was full and it was hard for me to talk over the lump in my throat.

"Will you go with me Sunday? To meet my family? It's long overdue."

"I would like that," I said. "But if you already have plans with someone…"

"Like I said, you're the one I want there with me."

I bit my lip and smiled over at him.

"Okay," I said. "I'll go with you."

Whatever he had been dealing with since lunch seemed to just slide away, at least for now.

We turned around and together walked home. Hand in hand.

"We have homework tonight," he said as the sun dropped over the horizon, leaving behind a swatch of oranges and yellows.

"Homework? What kind?"

"After we... I... move your things downstairs, we have to watch the movie, *Somewhere in Time*."

"I think maybe I saw it when I was young."

"I think you'd remember it if you did," he said.

"Sounds like I need to watch it again then."

A series of blasts from the ferry's horn announced that the last ferry of the night was leaving.

"There's a nighttime ferry?" he asked.

I shrugged. "I didn't think so. Maybe it's a Friday night thing."

Right now I wasn't too concerned with the ferry's schedule.

The owl greeted us as we neared the house.

"I really don't want to look up at the windows," I said.

"I know what you mean," he said. "You don't mind if I sleep on the sofa, do you?"

"I hoped you would."

And I wondered. Why would the ghost show herself to me?

The thought had occurred to me that the ghost might be my aunt. But that didn't quite fit. My aunt was older. The ghost was much younger.

And as far as I knew, my aunt had never loved anyone like Amelia had.

I hoped I was wrong about that.

I wouldn't want anyone to go through life and not feel this

swelling of love that I was feeling right now. My heart was overflowing. I wanted to hug the whole world. To shout my love for Cody from the rooftops.

CHAPTER 38
Cody

"I CAN'T BELIEVE we're actually here," Bailey said, turning around in a circle. "Christopher Reeve was right here."

We stood on the porch of the Grand Hotel, looking out over the gardens below.

Bailey was wearing her emerald green skirt with the side slit up to there, the white top, and the blue jean jacket. She was adorable.

"It is surreal, isn't it?" I said.

"I guess they let them bring cars on the island to film the movie."

"I guess so."

"I want to go to the Somewhere in Time festival. It's the end of October."

"That sounds like fun," I said, doing a mental calculation. I would still be here. I wasn't scheduled to go back to Houston until just before Thanksgiving. "We'll need to reserve our room soon."

She looked over at me with a funny expression.

"You've never been?"

"I've never gotten past the airport until this week," I said.

But now I wanted to do everything with Bailey. I wanted to go to the *Somewhere in Time* festival, the tours, everything.

I found it tragic that her aunt had lived here all those years and Bailey had never even so much as seen the movie.

Her face was bright with enthusiasm as we walked around the hotel, pointing out places we'd seen in the movie.

I was especially helpful with that, since I'd seen the movie several times with my Grandma Savannah. It was hands down her favorite movie. She and Grandpa used to come up here all the time. I was pretty sure they had gone to the *Somewhere in Time* festival at least once.

I would ask them tomorrow.

The orchestra began playing signaling that it was time for us to go into the main dining room for dinner.

"Shall we go into dinner, Milady?" I asked.

"I think you're mixing your time periods," she said, placing her hand in the crook of my arm.

"I hope you'll forgive me," I said. "I'm overwhelmed by your beauty."

She turned away, a little smile playing about her lips.

We reached the check-in desk.

"A reservation for Johnson," Cody said.

"Ah, yes," the older man said. "I have your table ready. Please follow me, Mr. and Mrs. Johnson."

Bailey looked over at me, her eyes wide. I just grinned.

"People make assumptions," I leaned over and whispered. "What can I say?"

And we did look good together. We looked like we belonged together.

The maître d' handed us our menus. "You must try the pecan balls," he said. "They're world famous."

"We will," I said. "Thank you."

"May I start you off with a glass of wine or champagne?" he asked.

"Champagne," I said.

"What, may I ask, are you celebrating?"

"Second chances," I said, grinning over at Bailey.

CHAPTER 39

Bailey

CODY SAT across from me at a table in the crowded Main Dining Room. The other guests were all elegantly dressed, some in early 1900s style. Apparently formal dress was a requirement to dine in the Main Dining Room of the Grand Hotel.

The high-backed fabric chairs were green and white striped. White table cloths. Waiters elegantly dressed in black tie attire.

Sparkly evening sunlight streamed in through the wall of windows with a gorgeously scenic view of Lake Huron, but it wouldn't be long before it was dark.

An orchestra played serene classical music, bringing the whole setting to life.

Cody had been right. If I had seen the movie, *Somewhere in Time,* I would have remembered it. It was one of those movies that had been made with pixie dust and carried an unforgettable magic.

There were so many things I recognized from the movie and so many things, of course, that I didn't.

Cody was a very knowledgeable tour guide about the whole thing. He denied having been here before and I believed him. He seemed as awed as I did as he spotted familiar landmarks.

He was wearing a black tuxedo. I had never seen him look so handsome as he did tonight.

And he was a perfect gentleman.

We had ridden in a carriage from our house to the Grand Hotel. A taxi, they called it. But I called it a magical carriage.

I felt every bit like Cinderella. And instead of feeling over-dressed as I had expected, I actually felt underdressed. My outfit was fine, but I knew what to wear next time.

I knew to wear something more formal. I had plenty of time to find the right dress before the festival in October.

Even though I had a house on the island, staying here in one of the rooms would be part of the whole experience. We could reserve a couple of rooms. I'd already done the calculations. Cody would still be here.

Would I? That was the beauty of having a reservation. It wouldn't matter if I had sold the house or not. I could still stay here.

But Cody was still be here, so I couldn't sell the house yet.

I sighed.

"Sounds like a deep subject for such a lovely setting."

"Sorry," I said. "I was just thinking."

"Would you like to share your thoughts?"

I shook my head and picked up a glass. "Not really. They aren't fully formed."

"I understand that." He held up his glass of the bubbling champagne. "To figuring things out."

Holding my glass up to his, I couldn't help but smile.

"Do you believe in time travel?" he asked.

"Maybe. But either way, I think the movie was written by a man."

"It was, actually. But why do you say that?"

"Because it didn't end right. They should have gotten together." I watched the bubbly wine in my glass.

"They did. Kind of."

I made a face. "He should have gone back in time and stayed there."

"That would have been a romantic ending."

I shrugged. "It's fiction. Why not make it happy and romantic?

"Good point," he said.

CHAPTER 40

Cody

I'D ALWAYS THOUGHT that *Somewhere in Time* had a happy ending.

I probably should have known that was just me being a guy since my grandma cried every time she watched it.

Apparently from a female perspective, it wasn't so happy.

As the sun inched its way over the horizon, we began our five-course dinner.

Shrimp dumplings were first.

"Have you ever had anything like this before?" Bailey asked after sampling the dumplings.

Maybe. "Not that I can remember."

"I haven't," she said. "I don't think we have food like this in the south."

The server brought out crusted whitefish next.

This was a whole new world for Bailey and I wanted to show her everything. I wanted her to experience everything.

I'd never been to the Grand Hotel. That much was true, but I'd been to places like this.

I wanted to share everything with Bailey. I wanted to show her the world.

And the thing was. I could show her the world.

I'd never thought about my life like this before.

I'd been raised to work hard just like everybody else. In fact, I had a strong work ethic. But I had been given opportunities that other people didn't. Doors opened to me that allowed me to make the most of what I had. And my grandparents were generous with what they had, sometimes to the disapproval of my parents.

I wanted to share everything I had with her like I had never wanted to share that part of my life before.

It was funny, I'd always just wanted to be ordinary.

"More champagne?" the waiter asked, coming to our table.

"For the lady," I said, putting a hand over my glass.

"Bottle to throttle," Bailey said, after the waiter walked away.

I held up a glass. "Bottle to throttle."

She sipped her wine in between courses.

"If you could go back in time, where... no... when would go?"

"That's easy," I said. "I'd go back six years ago."

"Is that so?" she said with a secret smile. "What would you do back six years ago?"

"Let me think," I said, leaning back in my chair. "I'd go back to that day I flew to College Station. The day I sat in my plane for an hour."

"Wait. What?"

She leaned forward, looking into my eyes.

"I flew right back out. I didn't even get out of the plane."

"Cody," she said. "When was that? Exactly."

"It was that fall. After I left. You would have been a junior."

"Why would you do that?" she asked, her voice barely audible over the music from the orchestra and the conversations swirling all around us.

Because I loved you.

"Because I didn't think you'd want to see me."

Sitting back, she looked away, not saying anything. I wanted to know what she was thinking. But I couldn't bring myself to ask.

I wasn't ready to tell her yet.

CHAPTER 41

Bailey

THERE WAS DANCING. And not just dancing. Waltzing.

Fortunately, I knew how to waltz. I had taken it as an elective my senior year. I had never, not even once, had the occasion to use my waltzing skills after that class.

It was almost like I had taken that class and learned to waltz simply for this moment.

Cody swept me around the room like he'd done this a thousand times. I didn't want to think about how he had become so skilled.

For just tonight, I wanted to think that I was the only girl he'd ever danced with.

Every girl was allowed that fantasy once in her life, surely.

And even if it wasn't true, he was here with me right now. Tonight.

The music changed into a slow song and the dance floor filled with those who wanted to just sway to the music.

Cody pulled me close and we did just that. Swayed to the music with our arms wrapped around each other.

Even as I fell even more in love with him, I wanted to tell him what an idiot he was.

That fall semester after he'd left, when I was a junior, was one of the worst times in my life.

Being at College Station had never felt right after he left and that semester, especially, was torture.

Everywhere I walked, I had memories of him. Of us.

Every time an airplane flew overhead, my heartrate would spin out of control and I would look up. Not that I would be able to see anyone in the plane, but I would look up, anyway. It was an involuntary reflex. I couldn't have stopped it if I'd wanted to.

I would have given anything to see him during that time. Anything to know that he thought about me. To think that maybe, just maybe, he missed half as much as I missed him.

By the time I went home to Dallas for the holidays, I had turned my sadness into mad. I was just mad enough that when he did call, I didn't answer.

I remembered the first time he'd called so well.

I'd been sitting at the mall with my parents. I'd stopped right there causing the person behind me to run right into me.

I'd just stood there, holding my phone, staring at his name on the screen.

"What's the matter?" Momma had asked, circling back. "You're in the way."

I hadn't cared.

But I hadn't answered Cody's phone call. And that had been the beginning of the end for me.

I hadn't deleted his number or even blocked it. I couldn't bring myself to do that.

Eventually he'd stopped calling.

I'd gotten a new phone when I moved back to Dallas, expecting all my numbers to transfer, but some of them hadn't. His was one of them.

If he had gotten out of that plane and came to my door that day, my life could have been so much different.

It almost seemed like a higher power had given up on us

getting ourselves back together and stepped in to make things happen.

To make things right.

Things were right.

I was in the beautiful Grand Hotel on Mackinac Island on a beautiful spring evening dancing in the arms of the man I had never expected to see again.

The man I had never stopped loving.

CHAPTER 42

Cody

"LET ME CHECK YOUR BELT," I said.

"You already checked it," Bailey said, looking at me with that vexed expression I loved so much.

"Never hurts to be safe," I said.

Even so, we were in the very safe Phenom. The flight path was filed. The weather was clear all the way from here to Houston. It was a perfect day for flying.

I checked her belt anyway and tried not to think about how easy it would have been to simply turn a little, lean in a few inches, and press my lips against hers. So easy.

But I needed to focus on the checklist. And I was determined to not rush. Reminded myself that it had only been four days since I'd walked back into her life.

As I taxied out to the runway and got into takeoff position, Bailey put on her headset and watched everything I did.

I used to talk to her when we flew together. I'd tell her everything I was doing. Whether she was listening or not I didn't always know. I'd never asked. But she was watching me as intently as she ever did.

I could have let her take the controls, but I'd flown by the book back then and the book said not to let anyone else take control of the airplane.

Nonetheless I was pretty sure she could have flown the plane, even landed it if she'd had to.

She was smart. I just didn't know whether or not she had enough interest to remember what I'd taught her.

Probably not now, since it had been six years.

"Ready?" I asked.

"Ready," she said with a little nod.

I got the plane into the air and took it for a little spin around Mackinac, over the Grand Hotel, over our… her… house.

We passed one of the ferries loaded with people as we headed out over Lake Huron. Bailey kept her face glued to the window the whole time.

Then I set the course for due south and we leveled off at ten thousand feet.

I could have easily gone higher in the Phenom and I might later, but for now, I wanted to let Bailey see the ground below. The houses. The cars on the roads. The rivers and lakes.

"All good?" I asked.

She nodded. Then she showed her hand.

"Isn't this Phenom rated for forty-one thousand feet?" she asked.

"What's that?" I asked, looking over at her. Surely I'd heard her wrong.

"Forty-one thousand. We're only at ten thousand."

"You want to go higher?" I asked.

She grinned. "Don't you?"

"Hold on," I said, making the adjustments to take us up to forty thousand.

Minutes later, we were cruising again. This time at a much higher level.

"Better?" I asked.

She nodded. "Nice view of cumulus clouds below us."

Wow. I felt an unexpected burst of pride.
She knew far more than I had given her credit for.
Now I most definitely wanted to kiss her.

CHAPTER 43

Bailey

I WATCHED as Cody silently went through the preflight checklist.

I followed along, keeping up with what he was doing.

Back in college when we had flown together, he had always talked out loud. I never really knew if he was doing it for my benefit or his.

Either way, I heard everything he said. He had never let me take the controls, but I felt like I knew enough that I could have gotten us on the ground. I knew the lingo. I knew all the steps for both takeoff and landing.

It was a little like waltzing. A skill I'd learned, but had never put to use. Only difference was Cody had taught me to fly, but never let me do it. Someone else had taught me to waltz and the only other person I'd waltzed with outside of class was Cody.

I was pretty sure I was thinking too much.

It's what I did, especially when I was nervous and I was nervous about meeting Cody's family.

I had no idea what to expect and he hadn't really given me any information. I knew that the barbecue was being held at his grandparents' house. His parents may or may not be there. His siblings may or may not be there. There could be cousins.

There was a lot of ambiguity and he didn't seem the least big concerned by it.

I shouldn't be concerned about it either. I knew that logically. But my heart said otherwise. My heart had made it important. I cared whether or not they liked me.

"Do you think your family will like me, okay?" I asked.

He glanced over at me with a confused expression.

"My family is going to love you."

He hadn't said anything, but I had figured things out. I had figured out that another girl was supposed to be there today.

That's all I knew or all I thought I knew.

I wouldn't ask and he wouldn't tell me and I didn't blame him. It wasn't any of my business.

Still. I hoped his family wasn't disappointed that he brought me instead of her. The other girl could be someone that his family had come to love.

"You're thinking too much," Cody said, his voice coming loud and clear through the headset.

"You're right," I admitted. "I'll stop."

I made an expression that was intended to look blank.

He just laughed. "You can't do it."

"I can," I insisted.

He just shook his head. "Your brain doesn't have an off button and you know it."

"Well. Who wants to turn their brain off?" I asked, while trying to take his words as a compliment.

A few minutes later, he caught me off guard.

"Do you want to take the controls?" he asked.

"What? No."

"Why not?" he asked. "I'm right here."

"It's been too long. I've probably forgotten."

"You don't forget," he said.

"I do," I said. "I could have."

"Where's the autopilot?" he asked.

"Right there." I pointed.

"You may have forgotten, but you remember more than most new pilots know."

"Okay," I said.

Anything to get me out of my own head, at least for a little while.

CHAPTER 44

Cody

I TOOK over the controls when it was time to land, even though I was convinced that Bailey could have done it.

It was comforting to know that if something happened to me or anyone else she was flying with, she would know what to do. But it was too soon to let her land. I needed to review some things with her first. If she was going to pilot a plane, she needed to do it right.

I took the plane in for a smooth landing, arriving earlier than planned.

Things were about to get interesting.

Grandpa had sent a car to pick us up. I saw his personal driver, Peter, waiting next to the black sedan. At least he hadn't sent a limo.

We had no luggage, so we didn't have to deal with that.

It was something of a shock stepping out into the humidity. Fortunately, it wasn't hot yet. The high today in Houston was supposed to be seventy-one. Good weather for an outdoor barbecue.

After helping Bailey to the ground, I spoke to the staff member who was there to service the airplane.

Then I took Bailey's hand and led her to the car.

"Good morning, Peter," I said.

"Good morning, Mr. Johnson," he said, opening the back door.

After Bailey slid in, I slid in next to her instead of going around to the other side.

"How was it?" I asked. "Your first flight?"

"Not bad," she said, but I could see the color in her cheeks. I had a feeling she thought it was better than she was letting on.

It had been obvious to me that she knew what she was doing. I had a new project. Teaching Bailey how to fly.

Traffic was light as Peter drove us down the Interstate toward Memorial.

I'd only been away for four days, but it seemed like a much longer time.

Probably because so much had happened.

I'd found Bailey. That was the main thing.

Not to mention the ghost in her aunt's house that was now her house.

It was still surreal that of all the places Betty could have found for me to live during my stay in Mackinac, she'd picked Bailey's house.

No one would ever be able to convince me that it wasn't more than chance. It was fate.

Things like that didn't happen randomly.

The world was too big.

I took Bailey's hand as we entered my grandparents' neighborhood.

The only thing I was worried about was her being mad at me for not telling her who my grandparents were.

I reminded myself, again, that I'd had no reason to.

Just as she hadn't taken me home to meet her family.

Our world in college had consisted of just the two of us.

Well, now I was expanding that world. I was bringing family into it.

Things would be different now.

But if I was going to keep her, it had to be done and the sooner the better.

Peter pulled into the circle drive and came around to open the door.

"You're here, Sir," he said, unnecessarily.

"Thank you, Peter."

I held onto Bailey's hand as we walked along the sidewalk to the front door.

It was only after we were almost to the door that I realized there weren't any cars. We weren't early, so it wasn't that.

"Do you know if they're home?" I asked Peter over my shoulder.

"Yes sir," he said. "They're expecting you."

Very odd. I would have heard if anything had happened.

But everything seemed calm. Butterflies fluttered about in my grandmother's colorful flowers and birds flew to and from the bird feeder Grandma kept hidden behind one of the shrubs, allowing her to attract birds she could watch from inside the house.

Well, whatever it was, at least my grandparents were here.

I went up to the front door and it opened before I could knock.

My grandmother answered the door.

CHAPTER 45
Bailey

I HADN'T KNOWN what to expect.

I certainly hadn't expected to be embraced by Cody's grandmother or to be greeted so warmly.

"It's so nice to finally meet you," she said. "Cody used to talk about you all the time."

"He did?" I asked, looking over at Cody.

"The downside to meeting my family," he said, leaning close in a mock whisper.

"Yes," Grandma said with a daring grin. "You will now learn the real truth."

We walked through a large foyer with sparkling clean shiny stone floors. A wide staircase led up to the second floor and big open two-story windows let in the warm morning sunlight.

An oversized grandfather clock, steadily ticking away the minutes, stood tall and regal next to the stairs.

We turned left into a family room that was both magazine lovely and invitingly comfortable at the same time.

A large sectional in an off-white fabric invited people to sit in front of the gas fireplace. Even though it wasn't cold, the fireplace burned low, the coals glowing and the flames barely licking the logs. It looked about as real as any wood burning fireplace could.

A seal-point snowshoe cat lay curled up on a soft looking pet pillow in front of the fireplace. Probably why it was on.

The coffee table had a couple of magazines on it and another cat, a big solid white flame-tipped one, lay stretched out across the magazines, watching us with slitted eyes.

I didn't see a television. Instead, there was an abstract painting hanging over the fireplace.

The room had two walls of windows on opposite sides. One side looked out over the perfectly manicured lawn, the opposite side looked out into an enclosed courtyard. The courtyard had a fire pit, a table, and several outside lounge chairs.

We walked through the family room into the very clean, very modern kitchen. Marble countertops, shiny white cabinets with clean lines—no knobs. Nothing on the counters except for a wooden cheese tray and a pretty green ivy in one corner in front of the window. I didn't recognize the brand of appliances, all in black.

"Grandpa is out back," she said, "getting the grill ready."

"Where is everybody else?" Cody asked.

"They might stop by later. Have a seat," she said to me. "Cody. Go out and see if Grandpa needs anything."

Cody hesitating, looking over at me.

"Go on," Grandma said. "We'll be fine."

I watched Cody walk away as I slid onto a bar stool at the island.

Cody's grandmother did not look anything like anybody's grandmother.

She was dressed much as I was. A light green gauzy skirt and a matching cardigan set in a lightweight cashmere. Her shoulder-length hair was pulled back in a barrette at the back of her head.

She sat down next to me and smiled at me with a radiant

smile that reflected what could only be happiness that radiated from deep within.

"Are you a vegetarian or a vegan?" she asked.

I shook my head.

"If you are, just tell me. I have one daughter who's a vegetarian and one who's a vegan. We can accommodate any dietary restrictions."

I smiled back. "I can eat just about anything."

"You're like Cody," she said, then kept talking, not giving me time to even think about getting uncomfortable. "Cody loves Mackinac Island. He sent us some pictures he took these past few days. Are you planning on living there or going back to Dallas?"

"I haven't decided yet," I said. "It was a shock when my aunt left me the house."

"I can only imagine." She looked at me sympathetically. "If you ever need to talk about it, please feel like you can talk to me. I'll give you my phone number before you leave today."

I was shaking my head. "I wouldn't want to bother you. I know you're busy." Cody had told me that his grandmother still worked as a psychologist with several regular patients.

"I know you just met us," Grandma Savannah said. "But you'll soon see just how important family is to us. Family first before anything else."

"I come from a very small family," I said. "No brothers or sisters."

"Well," I said. "We have enough in our family that no one ever has to feel like they have to go through anything alone."

"Cody's very fortunate," I said.

"Yes. He is." She smiled. "Now," she said. "You can help me carry a couple of trays outside."

I waited while she pulled covered plates out of the refrigerator and put them on a couple of larger trays. Tomatoes. Lettuce. Pickles.

Then together we carried them outside to the table where

Cody stood with his grandfather next to the humongous gas grill.

He smiled when he saw me coming out the door and went over to take the tray from my hands to set it on the table, even though it wasn't heavy and had handles.

"You okay?" he asked, leaning close.

"I'm fine," I said with a smile.

And I really was. Grandma Savannah made me feel welcome and not even a little out of place. In fact, I was feeling quite at home.

CHAPTER 46

Cody

"I DIDN'T THINK I would ever see her again," I said, snapping the lid off a water bottle.

Grandpa grunted, something that sounded like something between agreement and no comment. He was bent over the large barbecue grill, meticulously scraping the grates with a stiff wire brush.

I stood in my grandparents' backyard, a light breeze toying with the delicate pink flowers of the mimosa tree near the house, the sun warm on the back of my neck.

Grandpa finished up brushing the grates of the preheated barbecue grill, then put away the brush and turned to look at me.

"How long's it been since you looked for her?" he asked.

"How long?"

He shrugged and twisted the cap off his own bottle of water. "Yeah. How long?"

I thought back. How long had it been since I had looked for Bailey? I had a social media account, but it wasn't something I used every day.

Bailey Winters was a frequent search, but I never failed to come up empty or with someone obviously not her. Google pulled up lots of Bailey Winters, but never the right one. I had decided she must have gotten married and changed her name.

"A year, maybe," I said. "Give or take." Had I googled her last week? I couldn't remember.

"I see," he said. "And it's been six years since you saw her?"

"Right at."

I glanced back over toward the door. Grandma would be kind to her. I knew that. But I didn't like abandoning her even for a few minutes.

"Go tell your grandmother I don't need anything," he said.

Just then the back door opened and Grandma and Bailey stepped out, both carrying trays.

"Are you okay?" I asked, leaning close to Bailey so only she could hear me.

"I'm fine." She smiled that radiant smile that never failed to cause my heart to race at Mach speed.

I pulled out a chair. "Have a seat," I said. "Grandpa, this is Bailey."

"It's a pleasure to finally meet you, Bailey," Grandpa said. "I've heard a lot about you."

Bailey glanced at me, then back. "Really?"

"Since Cody was in college," Grandma said.

"How do you like your burger?" Grandpa asked.

"Well done," I said. "extra tomato, pickles, and onions. No mustard."

All three of them looked blankly at me.

I shrugged. "I have a good memory for things like that."

"Indeed you do," Grandma said, looking at me with that shrewd look she sometimes got in her eyes, usually when she had just figured something out.

I sat down next to Bailey while Grandma went over to say something to Grandpa.

"I thought your whole family was coming," she said.

"I think they decided to break you in easily."

"Break me in?"

"My family can be overwhelming." I handed her a bottle of water.

"They didn't have to do that," she said, then looked pointedly at me. "Why would they think they needed to do that?"

I swept a lock of hair off her forehead and looked into her beautiful green eyes. Eyes that reminded me of a field of Kentucky bluegrass.

"Because you're important to me," I said.

CHAPTER 47
Bailey

I WOKE up just as Cody lowered the landing gear as we approached the lighted Mackinac airport runway. Sometime while I slept, it had gotten dark.

"Hi," Cody said. "We're almost home."

I nodded, looking ahead at the little runway that was barely visible. If I hadn't known it was a runway, I probably wouldn't have even noticed it.

It was definitely an interesting way to wake up.

"Sorry I fell asleep," I said.

"No need to apologize, Chère," he said. "It was a long day."

I straightened up in my seat and put on my headset.

"Your grandparents are amazing," I said, smiling over at him.

"I agree. Next time, you'll meet more of the family."

I smiled in the darkness. "Good," I said.

Whenever he said *next time*, my heart did a little flutter. I wanted there to be a next time. And a next time. And a next time.

He took the airplane in for a smooth landing, then taxied over to the parking area.

A horse-drawn taxi waited for us near the terminal. The

horse was obviously used to being near airplanes since it barely twitched.

We stepped out of the airplane in significantly colder weather than when we'd boarded the airplane in Houston.

I shivered. "It's cold," I said.

"The low tonight is twenty-nine," he said.

"Wow. That's a lot different from Texas in May."

"It is." He slipped on a pair of gloves. "I have to secure the airplane."

"Okay," I said. "I'll wait."

The terminal was obviously closed, so I didn't really see another option.

"I'll hurry," he said.

And he was true to his word. A few minutes later we were tucked in the horse taxi, blankets around us.

"Not so bad now, is it?" he asked.

"No." I looked up at him. "Not so bad."

As the horse taxi started moving, he wrapped his arms around me and touched his forehead to mine.

I leaned my head against his shoulder and my heart sighed. I hadn't thought I would ever be here in his arms again.

But fate had taken care of it. Fate had brought us back together after all these years. After what seemed like impossible odds.

The steady clip clopping of the horse's hooves was soothing and romantic as we followed the moonlit road leading into town.

As we neared the Mackinac Hotel area, there was an increase in traffic—foot traffic and horse taxi traffic. And we could see the lake from here, too.

"It's beautiful," I said, softly.

"Bailey," Cody said, nudging me up so he could look into my eyes. "Will you go steady with me?"

I looked blankly at him, then laughed for just a second before I realized he was serious.

"What?"

"We could take our time and work our way into a relation-ship," he said, talking quickly now. "But I don't want to risk losing you again."

We were facing each other now, the cool wind coming off from the lake, tousling my hair. I shoved it back with my hand.

"I know it sounds silly," he said. "But—"

"Yes," I said.

"Yes? It sounds silly?" he looked at me as though he didn't quite believe me.

"Yes," I repeated. "I'll be your girlfriend."

Then just to mess with him, I held out my hand for a handshake.

"Oh, no," he said with a little chuckle. "we're not sealing that deal with a handshake."

"No?" I said, biting my lip to keep from smiling.

"Surely you've had time to think about it," he said.

I laughed. I couldn't help it. "Yes. I've had time to think about it."

He had his forehead against mine again.

"Bailey," he said, the words coming out on a soft breath.

Then I tilted my head up just a little. Just enough.

And his lips touched mine, taking my breath away.

And everything else ceased to exist. It didn't matter that we were in one of the most beautiful places in the world. It was just me and this man.

Sealed with a kiss.

CHAPTER 48

Amelia

AMELIA STOOD LOOKING at the painting of her and Carlton done just after their wedding. They had been so young. So in love.

The stars were bright tonight. Not as bright as they had been in the 1800s, what with all the electricity lighting up everything at any given moment, but the sky still carried the loveliness of Mackinac Island.

She stood at the window of her bedroom. Bailey's room now. And watched as the taxi carriage brought Bailey and Cody home.

They stood in the moonlight, arms wrapped around each other, after the carriage drove off and looked out over the lake.

She watched as they gazed toward the moonlight reflecting off the water.

Then he gently placed a hand on her cheek and kissed her.

Amelia had had one job to do and it was done. It had been so easy.

Cody and Bailey were so obviously in love with each other.

They had really done it all themselves, but she had helped where she could. Little things. Unplugging the landline so she'd be surprised when he showed up and wouldn't have the chance to leave before he got here. Showing herself in Bailey's bedroom to get her downstairs with him. That hadn't helped much, but that was okay.

Amelia had thought getting Bailey downstairs would seal the deal, but it had taken something else. Something only they knew.

So Amelia could go. She would miss this old house. But spending eternity with Carlton was her reward.

Bailey and Cody turned and hand in hand, they looked up at Amelia. They doubtless expected to see her, since they had seen her here before.

She had to let them know that she was going. That they didn't have to look for her any longer.

She held up a hand, then slowly faded away.

Her work here was done.

Epilogue

BAILEY

October

I **STOOD** in my suite at the Grand Hotel and turned this way and that in front of the full-length mirror. I was wearing the perfect 1912 dress. It was a long floor-length straight skirted dress in an embellished silver and white. The skirt reminded me of a floor-length pencil skirt, except it was easier to move around in.

The bodice was high neck, the sleeves stopped just below my elbows. The wide sash in dark gray, looped around my waist like a cummerbund, was tied in a bow in the back.

My hands were covered in long white gloves. I wore a matching hat and carried a delicate parasol that might protect my skin from the sun, but wouldn't survive in the rain.

It was perfect.

I left my room and walked to the end of the hall. Cody stood there, waiting for me. He, was dressed in a 1912 suit.

"Milady," he said, holding out an arm for me.

"You're mixing your time periods," I said.

"I know," I said. "but it's part of my charm."

I rolled my eyes at him, but I couldn't keep from smiling

Cody Johnson, grandson of Noah Worthington, had nothing if not buckets of charm.

Minutes later, standing in the lobby of the Grand Hotel, surrounded by people dressed similarly to us, an orchestra playing in the background, I felt like I had traveled back over one hundred years in time.

"We're in 1912," Cody said as we stood there in the middle of the lobby, people flowing around us.

I smiled up into his sky-blue eyes.

If Cody wanted me to travel to 1912 with him, I would do it. I would travel anywhere with him.

I wouldn't tell him that, of course.

"No," I said, teasingly. "You traveled to 1912 to be with me."

"I'll follow you to the end of time, Chère. Just lead the way." He removed his hat and kissed me lightly on the lips—a kiss befitting that of a married couple in 1912. Well, maybe a little more risqué than allowed in 1912, considering we were in public.

I smiled to myself. There was indeed magic on Mackinac island and now I was indelibly part of it. Or maybe, more accurately, it was indelibly part of me.

Cody and I, together, created the magic.

We had a home here and a life here together.

But no matter where we were, we would be together forever. Just like Amelia had waited for Carlton, I would wait for Cody if I had to.

We had made an agreement.

Sealed with a kiss.

Keep Reading for a preview of KISS ME AT MIDNIGHT…

KATHRYN KALEIGH

Kiss me at MIDNIGHT

THE WORTHINGTONS

Chapter 1
Kendal Johnson

"PREPARE FOR LANDING." The words were quick and perfunctory. Not even necessary. It was obvious we were descending in altitude.

The clunk of the wheels dropping interrupted the steady roar of the Phenom private airplane.

Unfortunately, the cumulonimbus clouds blocked the view of New York City I had been looking forward to seeing as we flew in over the city.

The pilot, my older brother Mason, fearlessly took the plane right down into the heart of the rain storm. According to the radar as reflected on my phone's weather app, he had no choice if we were going to land at Teterboro Airport in the next… two days.

I caught myself holding my breath as we traveled through the clouds. It was like flying through darkness. It was always a bit disconcerting to be in the air with absolutely no visibility.

Even on a clear night, lights were visible on the ground below. But not in the clouds. The clouds were blindingly dark.

There was radar, of course, and normally I would be sitting in the copilot seat, watching everything… the computer screens and the runway as it came into view and hearing everything… the chatter coming through the headset over the radio and my brother's quickly uttered statements. I could fly the airplane if I had to. Not that I wanted to or would do it on purpose. But if something happened to the pilot, I could get us on the ground. A girl could hardly grow up being Noah Worthington's granddaughter and not learn her way around a cockpit.

But today Mason brought his new wife Chloé. An opportune time for them to have a spontaneous weekend trip in New York.

I might be a little bit envious. Who wouldn't be? But Mason and Chloé were so happy, it was impossible to not be happy for them.

I forced my attention away from the blindingly opaque clouds to stare at the radar on my phone. I could see that there were no other planes near us. Still. I held my breath.

A text came though from my best friend, interrupting my intense scrutiny of the radar images of the area around us.

JULIA: *Have you landed yet?*

I smiled. Julia had the patience of a rabbit.

ME: *I will let you know. I promise.*

Julia and I had been best friends in college. Columbia University. We had both majored in accounting. Now I worked in accounting. She didn't. She owned her own clothing store and had a line of clothes she had designed herself. I don't think she had even so much as touched a spreadsheet since graduation. She'd certainly never touched a tax form, not even her own.

With her daddy being a writer and her mother being a neurosurgeon, she didn't have to. More than a bit spoiled, she sailed through life like it had been cut from whole cloth just for her.

In college, she and I had dated brothers. She dated Joshua and I dated Thomas. I had dated Thomas longer than she had dated Joshua.

Yet in two days, Julia would be Mrs. Mitchell.

I stared out the window and forced away the surge of emotions that came with that thought. I was happy for her. Truly I was. I had to be. I was one of her maids of honor. An honorary maid of honor, she called me. Her older sister was her actual maid of honor and since both of them lived in New York, bore the weight of the title.

Fortunately, Thomas would not be at his brother's wedding. From what I'd heard through the grapevine, he was piloting international commercial flights with a grueling schedule. That's how it was being a commercial pilot. Being a pilot didn't have to be grueling. There were other jobs, but he chose grueling.

I was mostly over being mad at him for making that choice, although I honestly still didn't understand why he had chosen it.

It had been eight years since I had seen Thomas, but a day didn't pass when I didn't think about him in some form or fashion. Maybe just a fleeting thought. Or I'd see someone who reminded me of him. I'd hear someone talking who sounded like him.

My grandfather had added a third floor to his private terminal for offices. There were four spacious offices on that floor, but they were all open, giving me an unparalleled view of the waiting area for passengers on the second floor. I had moved my desk so that I could not only hear what was going on downstairs, but I could watch people come and go. I could have put my desk in front of the window overlooking the tarmac, but the people in the waiting area were overall more interesting to me. With nothing but numbers to keep me company at my computer, I welcomed the distraction.

As the plane broke out of the clouds, sliding beneath them, rain pelted the plane, slamming against the windows.

Mason was a good pilot, but flying in the rain wasn't my favorite. I preferred clear blue skies with cumulous clouds.

Then I saw it. The Empire State Building. Even in the rain, it stood tall and proud.

I didn't have to check a calendar to know what today was. I knew exactly what day it was.

September 13.

Just two days to go.

In two days, it will have been exactly ten years since the day Thomas and I met at Columbia University as first year freshmen.

We hadn't chosen the Empire State Building for its romantic aspect, at least not completely. The first movie he and I had seen together was King Kong.

That's why we had chosen September 15 and the Empire State Building.

September 15. This year.

I was certain he had forgotten about it.

It wasn't the kind of thing a guy would remember.

But I remembered.

Chapter 2
Thomas Mitchell

The only thing good I could say about this trip was that I was traveling first class.

I felt every sway and turn of the large commercial jet. We were in autopilot now. The pilot that had taken us off the ground, I had decided, was an experienced pilot. Takeoff had been smooth and we had left the Paris airspace with practiced precision.

The eight-hour flight from Paris to New York could have been worse. Maybe.

I sat next to a young lady with long blonde hair who was objectively pretty. She had long lashes and plump lips. She was model thin. All those were good things in a young lady.

But she kept looking over at me with overt flirtation in her eyes and obviously someone had failed to tell her that wearing heavy perfume on a commercial jet was contraindicated. Not that her perfume bothered me, necessarily, but if she had been sitting next to anyone other than me, it might have been a problem. I'd seen that happen one time too many.

I should have taken the time to change out of my pilot's uniform, not that it would have mattered. But the uniform tended to capture women's attention and Lucy—I'd heard the flight attendant call her name—was no exception.

I had been running late and I couldn't afford to miss this flight. Not if I wanted to make it to my brother's wedding. There was no way I was going to let my only brother get married without me there. It was just the two of us and we had always been there for each other through thick and thin.

I forced my attention back to the novel I was reading— trying to read—on my iPad. I'd read the same paragraph three times. I usually got through a whole novel on one of these international flights, but oddly enough, the cockpit was a whole lot less distracting than the cabin, even first class.

I shifted, again, turning toward the window, but instead of reading, I found my thoughts wandering just as my attention had.

I flew in and out of New York several times a week and had even visited my sister there. Our parents had moved to Florida a few years ago to one of the tried and true retirement communities on the beach. Loved it. It would have stifled me.

Other than that, I hadn't spent any time of any consequence in New York since the day I had walked across the Columbia University stage, diploma in hand.

I knew the moment the pilot took the plane out of autopilot. Maybe I didn't *know* know, but I knew. An experienced commercial pilot knew the drill.

I was so rarely a passenger and I hoped I didn't have to be a passenger again anytime soon.

A familiar chime sounded and the fasten seatbelt light came on. My blonde seat mate put her seatbelt back on. I hadn't taken mine off. I never flew without my belt fastened. Usually a five-point harness. Nonetheless, I reflexively checked the belt. Tightened it a little bit. I had to admit I felt a bit exposed without the five-point harness.

We were still above the clouds, but it would be raining when we landed. Not the most pleasant New York welcome.

When I had moved out of New York, I had moved out completely. I had bought a condo up in Boston and that was where I still lived. I hadn't been home enough for it to ever really seem like a home. Besides, a home was a place where someone was waiting for you to come home. No one waited for me to come home.

Staying in New York would have been too hard. And since my reason to stay there hadn't panned out, I had moved away. To say that I had moved on might be a stretch. Moving on implied that I had forgotten the reason I had moved away.

And yet I knew exactly what today was. I knew that September 15 was in two days.

It seemed like an arbitrary date. September 15.

But it was September 15, twelve years since the day, give or take, that I had met Kendal Johnson. That had been one of the best days of my life. Probably the best.

And somewhere along the way, we had made a pact.

A pact that she had probably forgotten all about. She would have no reason to remember it.

It had been made long before we had gone our separate ways.

I hadn't seen her since graduation day eight years ago. After graduation, we had simply said goodbye and I had watched her walk away, disappearing into the fold of her family.

There was some comfort in that. Comfort that she wouldn't be alone. The comfort was hollow, however.

That had been one of the worst days of my life. Probably the worst.

Chapter 3
Kendal

Julia was waiting for me inside the private terminal. Squealing when she saw me, she ran up and hugged me. She had her fiancé with her.

After Julia let me go, Joshua took my hands and looked at me in that intense way he had. Seeing him had me feeling a little unsettled. He and his brother Thomas didn't look alike, exactly, at least not to strangers, but I'd always been able to see their resemblance.

Joshua's hair was lighter, almost blonde, but their eyes were so very similar. The same dark blue. Cerulean blue. But Thomas's had always been more attractive to me, at least. Part of it might have been that he had thicker eye lashes than his brother Joshua.

Or part—most—of it had been the way he'd looked at me. His gaze had always been like a promise. A promise that I was the only girl he would ever look at like that.

"You don't look any worse for wear," Joshua said.

"Stop it, Joshua," Julia scolded. "Just ignore him," she told me.

"It's been years since I've seen her," he said. "I just didn't know how she would fare as she approached thirty."

"Again," Julia said. "Just ignore him." She leaned forward

and whispered. "I think he's having some kind of mid-life crisis."

I looked at Joshua, then ignored him as Julia suggested and said. "He's only two years older than we are."

"He's over thirty though," she said.

"Too young for a mid-life crisis." I knew. I had uncles.

"Trust me," Julia said.

I looked from one of them to the other.

"And yet the wedding is still on."

"Eh." Julia shrugged.

"I can hear you," Joshua said. "I'm right here."

"It's a good thing you like older men," I said, deciding to mess with both of them. "Since you're about to marry one."

"Hey," Joshua said.

"Come on," Julia said, linking her arm with mine.

"My luggage," I said, looking over my shoulder.

Julia waved a hand. "It's probably already in the car. You're going to love our hotel room. We have a perfect view of the Empire State Building."

I only halfway listened to what she was saying after that.

The Empire State Building.

The words triggered a switch in my head—one that turned off all logical thoughts.

I'd never told anyone, not even Julia about my pact with Thomas. I knew that Thomas hadn't told it either. If he'd told his brother, then Julia would know. And Julia would have told me. She would have told me how stupid it was or else she would tell me how romantic it was. She was unpredictable like that.

I'd always considered Julia to be lucky. She and Joshua had stayed together while he went to graduate school and now he was a licensed psychologist.

In New York.

His job had not taken him away. Not like his brother.

Water under the bridge, I told myself as I stepped out into

the damp weather, beneath an awning, and climbed into the limo. Even though we were under shelter, the blowing rain splashed my raincoat.

"Where's your sister?" I asked as we settled in. Julia sat in the middle, me on one side and Joshua on the other. "I didn't think she'd let you out of her sight this weekend."

"Violet is tied up with details at the hotel." Julia barely refrained from rolling her eyes. "She wants everything to be perfect."

"And don't you?" I asked with a little smile.

"Of course."

"Does she ever," Joshua muttered under his breath.

The windshield wipers fought against the blinding rain and a thunderclap followed a flash of lightning.

I liked a good thunderstorm just fine as long as I was inside, preferable curled up in front of a fireplace with a blanket and a good novel. Being out in the storm would not be my first choice. Once we reached the hotel, we shouldn't have to go out again since the wedding was in the hotel.

"We're having dinner at that steakhouse tonight," Julia said. "The Eastside Grill."

"The one near the university?" I asked.

"Yes," Julia said happily. So much for not having to go back out in the storm and according to the radar the rain wasn't scheduled to let up until morning and then only for a few hours. The weekend promised to be a rainy one. I didn't tell her though. This was her wedding and a little bad weather shouldn't be allowed to ruin it.

"If Thomas could be here, it would be like old times," Julia said.

I didn't answer. I really couldn't. My thoughts were scrambled again.

"Sorry." She winced.

"No," I said. "You're right. It would be like old times."

I had decided that I would not act weird about Thomas. It

was certainly helpful that he wouldn't be here. Facing his family, watching his brother marry my best friend would be torture enough. Not having to see him would definitely make it easier.

Besides, Julia was ecstatic. More so than her usual enthusiastic state. If her life had indeed been cut from whole cloth just for her, she actually appreciated it. I'd rarely ever heard her complain. Entitlement was not in her repertoire.

"Anyway," Julia said. "I decided that you and I would share a room tonight and tomorrow night."

"Oh?" I hadn't expected to be sharing a room. I shouldn't be surprised though since we'd shared the same dorm room for four years.

"Where are you going for the wedding night?" I asked. It wasn't that I cared, but it seemed like something that a maid of honor would know.

"Joshua won't tell me."

"Really?" Leaning forward, I looked past her over at Joshua. "You're a brave man."

He grinned and my heart lurched. That grin reminded me of Thomas. Were they looking more alike as they aged or had I just not realized their resemblance until now?

Once again, I sent up a word of thanks that Thomas wasn't going to be here. I didn't think my heart could take it.

"I have to start this marriage off on the right foot," Joshua said. "Being the man and all."

Julia and I both just looked at him without comment.

"That was a joke," he said, looking at Julia.

"Of course, it was, honey." Julia patted him on the leg.

"Midlife crisis," she whispered to me in a stage whisper.

I laughed. It was so good to see my friends.

Maybe this weekend would pass by without any drama.

Keep Reading KISS ME AT MIDNIGHT…

Kathryn Kaleigh writes sweet contemporary romance, time travel romance, and historical romance.

kathrynkaleigh.com

SPOOK